THE BEST POLISH RESTAURANT IN BUFFALO

The Best POLISH RESTAURANT IN BUFFALO

A NOVEL BY

WILLIAM KOWALSKI

"This is a big old-fashioned book in every possible way.... Often funny, at times aching — a fine beginning to launch a novelist."
(*Brooklyn Bridge Magazine*)

"A grand debut. Eddie's Bastard is a beguiling blend of narrative *con brio*, human-heartedness, and zany surprises."
(Gail Godwin, author of *Evensong*)

FOR SOMEWHERE SOUTH OF HERE

"Has all the bravado of a bar stool reminiscence.... Kowalski's characters could be escapees from a Kerouac novel."
(*The New York Times Book Review*)

"Kowalski is a talented and vivid stylist." (*Washington Post*)

"Kowalski's graceful, almost lyrical style moves along briskly and elegantly, ensnaring the reader in the atmosphere of Santa Fe."
(*Providence Sunday Journal*)

FOR THE ADVENTURES OF FLASH JACKSON

"Kowalski has created an enduring character in Haley Bombauer, a.k.a. Flash Jackson, one we won't easily forget."
(*Rocky Mountain News*)

"An appealing and original story." (*Kirkus Reviews*)

"This poignant and entertaining novel resonates with homespun wit and truth." (*Booklist*)

"A coming-of-gender story." (*Library Journal*)

The Best Polish Restaurant in Buffalo
First Edition
Copyright © 2017 by William Kowalski
https://williamkowalski.com
https://best.polish.restaurant

Published by Orchard Street Books, in connection with Wordless Press.

Cover and text design by Sari Naworynski.

Edited by Peggy Hageman.
https://peggyhageman.com

Copyedited by Marianne Ward.
https://marianneward.ca/

ISBN: 978-0-9958943-0-3

For A.L. and J.C.

*The modern Polish joke has its origins in the anti-Polish
sentiment that took root in Germany during the
Third Partition of Poland, in 1795. Mockery of the Poles
was encouraged by the authorities in order to justify the theft
of an entire nation. You wouldn't take the land of someone
you regarded as an equal. But you had no problem stealing
from someone if you thought they were less than human.*

—Excerpted from *A Cultural History of the Polish Joke*,
the PhD thesis of Witold "Whitey" Lubek

1. STEERAGE CLASS (MAY 1908)

There were no words in Aniela's native Polish dialect to describe the stench in steerage.

Such an unnatural reek, as far as she knew, had never existed before in the history of the world. It was an affront to all humanity. Livestock, vomit, unwashed bodies, fetid breath, soiled clothing, bad food, devilish machines creating unholy smells, and not a breath of a breeze to blow any of it away: it was a smell so bad that it had convinced her, just one day into their journey across the Atlantic, that she, her mother, and her sisters had made a horrible mistake by leaving home.

She knew lots of words for smells, all right. There was the smell of *kielbasa* boiling in the iron pot over the fire in the old stone hearth, along with potatoes and wild herbs. There were the odors of horse and oxen manure in the road—highly distinct from the stink of her father's and brothers' thunder jugs, which she had to empty every morning so that their lordships would not be unduly put out by having to do it themselves. There were smells of vodka-and-onions on the breath

1

of faces pushed too close to hers, of the priest's unwashed stale clothing, of the beeswax candles that burned at Our Savior's feet every Sunday morning.

It was as if she was a nature girl, part animal, maybe, some kind of creature that defined the world by the scents it gave off. Sometimes memories of odd smells even crept into her head unbidden, and that was why she suddenly remembered that once, just a few years ago, there had been the disappointing smell of the ermine furs that the *szlachcianka* wore as she swept grandly through the village, within inches of Aniela's nose.

That had been a strange day. Under an alignment of the stars that not even the wisest old woman in the village could have predicted, the szlachcianka's grand carriage had stopped directly in front of the astonished Aniela as she was running an errand for her mother, right there on the main street, where everyone could see. That in and of itself was a piece of good luck. It was not every day that a poor girl like her got to see someone so grand. It would be something to tell her family about when she returned home. She was already memorizing the details to repeat later: *The carriage was black. It was pulled by a white gelding and a roan. The driver wore a fancy jacket with embroidery on the collar. There was mud on the left sleeve.*

Fortune continued to unfold as the carriage door opened and the lady herself exited, assisted by the gloved hand of her hired man. By this time, Aniela was so surprised she could do nothing more than stand with her mouth agape. She had never been this close to nobility before. *She walked like royalty. Furs on her shoulders. Her man held her dress out of the mud for her. She did not look to the left or to the right, but only straight ahead, like she didn't care about anything.*

Things became even stranger when the lady stopped on her way into the shop, the front door of which Aniela herself was blocking, due to her own clumsy farm-girl absent-mindedness, until she remembered to bend one knee in a rarely-used curtsy and step out of the way. She half-expected the footman to cuff her on the side of the head, or at least to hear angry words.

But the footman didn't even notice her, and the szlachcianka was not angry. She paused, one booted foot on the step, and she looked Aniela up and down.

Aniela was younger then, barely a woman yet, but the way this *pani* looked at her seemed to suggest she thought she was older than she actually was—a rival, or even a threat, perhaps.

That was ridiculous. Aniela would never think to compare herself to a woman who lived in a house separate from her animals, whose husband owned no less than four horses, who ate from china plates, who drank wine instead of vodka, who had a family pew at the front of the church—who was so close to God, in fact, that she even had her very own chapel on her estate, in case she didn't feel like worshipping amongst the great unwashed.

Yet the woman's stare was not unkind. There was even the hint of a smile about her face as she said, in haughty, refined Prussian dialect:

"This one imagines she's going places in life, doesn't she?"

That was when the smell of the furs had come to her nostrils, as the woman swept past. To Aniela's nose, they smelled just like what they were: the dead skins of dead animals, worn for show, devoid of life, possibly home to several different kinds of insects, and, like so many other things in life, rather disappointing when viewed up close.

Why had the szlachcianka said that about her? Aniela imagined no such thing about herself. She did not see herself as the kind of girl who would be going places. The furthest she could imagine was Poznań, a very long day's ride from the village. But why she would ever go there she could not begin to fathom. She had never been to Poznań—except when she was baptized, which of course she did not remember—and she had no desire or reason to go to there. Her entire life was there in the village, and on the farm just outside, where she lived with her parents, her three brothers, and her two sisters. Poznań had nothing to do with anything.

All the more reason, then, to be amazed at the latest turn her life had taken. For here she was now, in the hold of a ship that was the biggest thing she had ever seen, headed across the ocean for *Ameryka*, much farther than Poznań and infinitely more frightening. She shook her head to clear it, and looked around again in the gloom of steerage, surprised to find herself back here after her momentary flight back to Poland. Surprised…and disappointed. She didn't know exactly where in the world she wanted to be right now, but she was quite sure she didn't want to be where she was.

The ship itself was an experience never to be forgotten. It was so big that when she first saw it at the docks in Hamburg, she couldn't believe it was actually floating. It was ten times bigger than the biggest building she had ever seen, bigger than the cathedral in Poznań, which was, according to her mother, the largest thing on the earth. Only through a tremendous act of will had she managed to quell the terror she felt as they crossed the quivering gangplank and stepped onto the deck.

The ship bore the name of the man whom Poles hated more than the Devil himself: *Kaiser Wilhelm II*. It was a cruel twist of fate that the vessel should be named for the very person from whose clutches they were being delivered, the man who had decreed that all Poles were animals and should either be Germanized or put down like dogs. A bad omen, to be sure.

Aniela crossed herself and tried not to cry. She could hear her mother muttering under her breath, and she knew she was praying to St. Christopher, the patron saint of travelers. She had begun importuning this particular saint long before their journey began. The words failed to comfort her. They only served to convince her that something terrible was happening, for when else did anyone in her family pray out loud?

Her terror had grown as they were promptly ushered into the dank netherworld of the steerage hold. This was where they were to stay, they were told; they were not free to wander about the ship as they pleased, not even to get a breath of fresh air. That was a luxury reserved for the higher-paying passengers.

The crew of the ship was dreadfully rude to them while they were boarding, as if they had been paid nothing at all for passage, but were doing some great favor. That was all right; the peasants who crammed the hold were used to rudeness. They'd always been treated that way by the Prussians who had dominated their part of Poland for many years now, since the time of Aniela's great-grandparents and before. They knew not to react to such treatment. They didn't even waste energy resenting it, since there was nothing they could do to change it.

It was being trapped inside that Aniela couldn't stand. She wasn't used to being cooped up like a chicken. Immediately she felt the first pangs of fear, and her heart began to flutter against her ribcage.

This floating prison, she was sure, was the place where she would die.

She began to panic. At least she thought that was what was happening to her. Her breath came short and fast, and she felt like she was going to faint. This alone was even more frightening, for she was not the sort of girl who felt fear of anything much. And so her fear fed on itself, and it grew.

But eventually, common sense prevailed. Aniela was a very practical girl. She reasoned that there had been other ships in the history of the world, and that those ships had managed to float. She knew that this ship had crossed the ocean before, and so therefore it, too, could float. That had been demonstrated. They would not sell tickets on a ship if they knew it would sink.

Or would they? Perhaps it was all some elaborate Prussian plot to drown them. The Germans were always threatening to rid the world of their presence, after all.

No. She would not really believe it floated until she saw it with her own eyes.

And the smells. *Drogi Boże*, the smells.

They made their crossing in May. A storm had kicked up on their second day at sea, and raged for a day and a night. Now the ocean continued to toss. Those who hadn't been made ill by the constant up and down of the waves were sickened by the vomit that spilled from buckets and sloshed around the floorboards.

Because of that, few passengers had the stomach for the slop the crew served from the massive kettles at one end of the hold. Those who did have the strength to eat were often pushed out of line and forced to the back by the youngest and strongest men, who, with none of their own elders around to chastise them, had quickly taken to behaving like wolves. It was as if they were reverting to their animal natures. Well, what did one expect from men? They were scarcely better than the livestock. If you knew how to handle them, they were just as easy to manage. But if you let them think for one moment they could have their way, then have it they would. So you did not give them an inch of room. And if they insisted on behaving like animals, you treated them the way you did a recalcitrant beast: you beat them hard, you did not back down, and you never let them know they were stronger.

There were other hardships to contend with, too. The women had none of the privacy to which they were entitled. They had to do their business in buckets right out in the open, in front of the leering wolves. That kind of indignity was the normal state of affairs for Aniela, who had had to put up with worse from her brothers. That didn't make this any easier to bear, though. It only served to reinforce her opinion that no man was to be trusted, even for a moment, no matter how convincing he was.

Well, all except for Martyn. He was the baby of the family, and of all the boys he was the kindest, the sweetest, and the most easily tormented. He was the only one Aniela would miss, and she knew her sisters felt the same. Her mother had refused to weep when they left. But Martyn, fifteen years old, had cried openly as the wagon went down the road. It was a memory Aniela knew she would never be able to erase from her mind, no matter what.

The only blessing was that down here in the hold, it was hard to see. There were just three or four kerosene lamps. The only other light came through the portholes or down the hatches, and so everything was perpetually hidden in gloom, if not outright darkness. This was the only protection afforded their modesty.

Of course, darkness brought its own terrors, as any girl in this world of men knew all too well. They stayed together at all times, each one constantly checking to make sure the others were close by. They slept in shifts to ensure that no male dared try anything while they were asleep. They continued their prayers to St. Christopher, and they added new ones to St. Jude, the saint of lost causes, for by now they had begun to understand that their entire way of life was lost to them, and the odds against them surviving this journey were very great indeed.

The strangest thing of all about this ship was that everyone was mixed together: Poles, Jews, Ruthenians, Bulgarians, Slovenians, Slovakians, Hungarians, Romanians, Russians, Bohemians, Bavarians. They huddled together in tribes, dividing themselves naturally according to language and culture, glaring at each other with suspicion. Aniela had not known such a mélange of humanity existed, nor that all these languages existed, either. It was proof that the Biblical story of the Tower of Babel was true. Some of these people she had never even heard of.

She had seen Jews before, but she had never been this close to one, let alone whole families of them; she found herself observing them curiously, wondering if all the horrible things the priest had said about them were true. He had lied about practically everything else, after all, including his own divinity. These Jews appeared to be serious, grim people. They kept to themselves, and they regarded everyone around them with mistrust.

But then, so did everyone else. All in all, despite their funny locks of hair that curled down from the men's ears, and the strange clothing styles of the women, they did not seem so different.

Regardless of where they came from, they were all in the same boat now, Aniela reflected; and that was true in more ways than one.

Once they were out to sea, they were allowed on deck, but never more than an hour at a time. That, too, was a privilege reserved for the wealthier passengers. For the most part, the people in steerage had to rely on the hatches and the tiny portholes for fresh air, and those had to be closed in heavy seas. Imagine putting a cricket in a filthy cup and shaking it: that's how she would describe this journey to her best friend, Agnieszka, if she ever saw her again.

Which she wouldn't. Because Agnieszka was not going to Ameryka. And neither of them had gone to school long enough to learn how to write a whole letter to each other. So everything that happened to each of them from now on, for the rest of their lives, would remain a mystery to the other.

This thought only contributed to the great hole she had felt growing in her middle ever since their wagon had pulled out of the village, and which threatened to consume her whole being.

Aniela's mother, Zofia, lay on her bunk below Jadwiga, her elder sister. Aniela and her younger sister, Catarina, occupied the two facing bunks. Between them sat all the things they had brought from home, everything they could fit into one wagon. There were four flimsy wooden chests, one for each of them, plus a large steamer trunk. In the chests, each of them had put her most essential personal items: dresses, shoes, combs, and the like. In the trunk, Zofia had put certain things that no new home could do without: salt, earthenware bowls, a couple of knives, a large cooking pot with a lid, several hand-whittled wooden spoons, and other various and sundry implements. There were also several bits of white lace, handkerchiefs and doilies for the most part, which would serve no clear purpose but which had been too precious to leave behind. Their most valued possessions were an ebony crucifix and an image of Our Lady of Częstochowa, the Black Madonna.

That they had taken these items with them meant that their former home in the village was left without any holy images to protect it. But her father and brothers would not even notice. It would only be a matter of time before that house of men descended into total deviltry, Aniela knew. If they had left the lace behind, they would only have wiped their asses with it. She felt no guilt at abandoning them. Their decline had begun long before. She, her mother, and her sisters had set out on this path not because of any great ambition, but as a matter of survival.

In a small piece of crockery, covered carefully with oil-cloth, was the bubbling sourdough mixture that Zofia had taken from its place on the kitchen sill, and which she fed occasionally with a piece of bread or a bit of water. If she could manage to get it across the ocean without killing it, it would flourish in the new land. It would be a living piece of home that would always be with them.

That was what they would have to start their new lives in Ameryka: a few bits of clothing, some trinkets, two holy images, and the sourdough. Everything else had been left behind.

Which was, of course, the point of leaving in the first place. Not everything that was gone would be missed.

Better not to think about those things.

Curiously, Aniela felt immune to seasickness. Her mother and sisters groaned as if they were having their innards pulled from them. Whenever they felt the need, they simply leaned over the edge of their bunks and were sick upon the floor. The overflowing buckets had long ago lost their usefulness, and the women had lost all dignity. Zofia, whom Aniela had never seen display any sort of emotion before, prayed openly for death.

Other people in the steerage hold experienced even worse misery. A pregnant woman gave birth. The baby died. A day later, so did the mother.

The whole ship grieved. It seemed to all of them to be a symbol of everything everyone had given up, no matter where they'd come from.

All in all, this journey was worse than a nightmare. It was a living hell.

The szlachcianka's words came floating back to her suddenly: *This one imagines she's going places in life, doesn't she?* At the time, they had seemed like a taunt. Now they seemed like a prediction or an augury, such as one might read in coffee grounds or chicken entrails. Aniela didn't believe in practicing such things, because the priest said they were witchcraft. But she knew old women who did. And the words of the priest didn't stop her from knowing that their power was real.

The only good thing about this journey, in fact, was that no matter how bad it got, it would always be better than what they were leaving. The Prussians, her father, her brothers… all of it was behind her now.

Maybe now, in her sixteenth year, she could finally start to live.

2. KENMORE (SEPTEMBER 2015)

On Delaware Avenue, in the Buffalo suburb of Kenmore, a man named Iggy Podbielski stood in a parking lot with his hands on his hips, ruefully surveying the latest in a series of graffiti attacks on the wall of a certain building.

This building looked to be a veteran of such attacks. Its walls bore the faded scars of previous attempts by so-called street artists to beautify it with cryptic tags in spraypaint neon colors. The tags had been painted over many times, but always they bled through.

The result was an urban palimpsest. In a few centuries, Iggy thought, this wall might be a wealth of information to archaeologists trying to figure out what kind of place Buffalo had been.

But of him, there would remain not a trace. No one would remember his name, or that he had stood here. And if, by some miracle, they happened to find an old scrap of paper with the name Iggy Podbielski on it, a bill of lading or a receipt or something that had somehow survived the centuries unscathed, he would still mean no more to them than any old random Sumerian grain vendor whose thumbprint was still visible on a clay tablet, five thousand years after concluding his last deal.

Jesus, how depressing, Iggy thought, staring at this ugly graffiti. It made you wonder what the hell the point of anything was.

The building was an old place, by modern standards: it had stood there since 1951. It was just one story tall, but it spread out across nearly three thousand square feet. The exterior walls were fake stucco. They had begun to decay years earlier, the cement on the outside peeling away to reveal the rusted chicken wire underneath. A twenty-foot-tall lighted sign in the parking lot read ANGELA'S, but several of the letters had burned out a long time ago, so now it just said AN EL. Naturally, this was seized upon by every passing wit who thought he was the first to notice the similarity to a certain word pertaining to the human anatomy. Someone yelled it at him now, in fact, just another punk kid in a car:

"Anal!" the kid yelled. "Best food in town!"

Iggy didn't even bother looking. He just flipped a middle finger over his shoulder and continued to stare blankly at the graffiti.

Once upon a time, he would have cared enough about his public reputation to avoid such childish reprisals. But once upon a time, the restaurant wouldn't have looked this bad, either.

Once upon a time, the parking lot would have been full of cars, and there would have been a line of people out the door every Friday night for the fish fry. Once, this was the best

Polish restaurant in Buffalo, so good that even non-Polish people came there to sample the sausages, the cheeses, the pierogies, the smoked meat, the traditional breads and pastries. All kinds of people were welcome: Irish-Americans, German-Americans, Russian-Americans...even black people. That was the rule that had been laid down when the place was founded by his great-grandmother: Everyone welcome. She had known all too well what it was like to be excluded. When you saw blacks and whites rubbing elbows on Delaware Avenue, you knew you were in a special place.

And once upon a time, he would have had that sign fixed by now. But now, there was no point.

Iggy was forty-five years old, tall, stoop-shouldered, pot-bellied, jug-eared, and at the moment he was profoundly unhappy. Along with several family members, most of whom he was scarcely speaking to, he was the owner of the building that he was currently staring at. Iggy was a so-called businessman, an erstwhile chef, a former dreamer of dreams, a man of the people with no people around him, a family man with no children, whose wife would rather watch reruns of *Magnum P.I.* or Tom Cruise movies on the Internet all day than converse with him.

And at this moment, he was a very disappointed man—which was made worse by the fact that his disappointment was largely directed at himself.

Iggy was also the great-grandson of Angela, whose real name was Aniela. One hundred and seven years earlier, his great-grandmother had made the painful journey from Poland to start a better life. As had been explained to him approximately ten thousand times during his childhood, she had come to America because it was the place where anyone could get ahead if they worked hard enough. Free of the royal tyranny that had oppressed Europe for millennia, untainted by the endless strife between tribes, city-states, kingdoms, and nations, liberated from the classist oppression that made it impossible to rise above the station to which you were born, America was a magical place where the poorest peasant could create something from nothing.

Except, apparently, for his family.

It was the ruination of their American dream Iggy was staring at now.

Iggy had heard the American Dream lecture so many times as a kid that back then it was all he thought about. Anyone could make it in America if they just worked hard, everyone said—his parents, his uncles, his cousins, his grandparents, even his great-grandmother herself, who had lived to be ninety-eight years old. He had known her well, although he could barely understand her, since he didn't speak Polish and she had never had more than a passing acquaintance with the English language.

If you didn't make it in America, there was something seriously wrong with you. You just weren't trying. You didn't appreciate the sacrifice your ancestors had made on your behalf, leaving behind everything they held dear.

Nope. If you didn't make it, you were a failure—not just in business, but as a person, and in the eyes of all those who had come before you.

Iggy sighed and looked at the time on his cell phone. It was nearly time to start prepping for dinner.

Yes, despite the fact that the restaurant looked as if it was already in the late stages of returning to the earth from which it had sprung, it was still open. And he was determined that he would not close early. Angela's hadn't served its last meal yet. That moment was still three days away.

Iggy let himself into the kitchen through the back door. He flicked on the lights, listening automatically for the tell-tale scurry of little feet that would have indicated the presence of vermin. He heard nothing; he had always kept on top of the rat situation. The place might be going out of business, but it wasn't because of the health department.

He went to the sink and washed his hands up to his elbows. This was a ritual he performed at least two dozen times a day. Then he went to the cooler and thought about portions. How many people could he expect for dinner tonight? Probably none, he thought. People had simply stopped coming to Angela's. And that was why they were closing.

Why was that? He thought he knew. It was outmoded, outdated, badly marketed. They didn't even have a website. Iggy hadn't seen the point in one. His teenaged and adult nephews and nieces thought this was the most ridiculous thing they'd ever heard of. How were people supposed to find Angela's if it didn't exist on the Web? they said.

Same way they always had, Iggy replied. By looking in the phone book. Or driving by it. Or word of mouth. If you made good food, people would come.

But they made the same good food they always had, and nobody came. Iggy just didn't understand the Internet, apparently. He knew how to use e-mail and how to search for stuff on Google, but he could tell by the way the younger generation rolled their eyes and spoke to him with barely concealed impatience that there were entire levels of understanding of the online world that would always be beyond him.

The real problem, he felt, was that nobody wanted stodgy old Polish food any more. This wasn't 1950. It was 2015. People did not eat heaping plates of cabbage and egg noodles slathered with butter. They did not appreciate a platter piled high with steaming sausages. They did not like blood pudding or pig's brains or any of the other delicacies Iggy and his cousin, Brownie, knew how to prepare. Instead, they ate processed garbage from supermarkets and fast food restaurants; and there was nothing that a website could do about that.

Iggy heard the back door open behind him, precisely on schedule. He didn't need to turn around to see who it was, but he did anyway. It was Mr. Danny, the ancient baker, oldest surviving employee of Angela's, and possibly one of the oldest people in Buffalo. Because Mr. Danny was half-blind now, he was led in by his oldest son, Len. At nearly seventy, Len was an old man himself, an odd duck who rarely spoke to anyone and who'd never left his parents' home.

Mr. Danny was certainly over the age of ninety, though he was proud of the fact that he didn't know exactly when he was born. He had worked at the original Angela's since it had opened, nearly eighty years ago—back when it was still just a little bakery in Black Rock, before it had been expanded by Iggy's grandfather, Stanislaus, who was called Old Stosh in an attempt to distinguish him from the approximately twenty-five thousand other men named Stanislaus in the city of Buffalo.

Mr. Danny had started out as a dishwasher after dropping out of grade school, when he was probably between ten and twelve years old, gleefully thumbing his nose at whatever puny child labor laws might have existed then. He had never taken a vacation, either, except for the period that he still occasionally referred to as "that time I got drafted." That had been in 1942. Mr. Danny, who was just Danny then, had gone to Europe with the army during the Second World War, where he was trained as a cook. Upon his return to Buffalo, he took over the kitchen, and that was the role he had held for the next many decades.

Under the watchful eye of the Podbielski owners, headed by their matriarch, Aniela, Mr. Danny was the one who turned out the piles of steaming kielbasa links, the glistening pierogies, and the cabbage rolls that were all made from traditional Polish recipes, and which kept the people of Buffalo coming back, week after week. He was also in charge of all the baking, which had once formed a cornerstone of the business. In those days, with so many of the older people still having been born in the old country, Angela's was the best place to eat the food that reminded them of home. The war was over, those son-of-a-bitch Germans had finally had their asses handed to them once and for all, people had money to spend, and everyone who wasn't dead was in a more-or-less good mood.

All this had taken place long before Iggy was even born, of course; although he'd heard so many stories about those days, he felt as if he'd lived them himself.

Iggy wondered if Mr. Danny even knew that the place he'd worked at all his life was about to close. He wasn't sure how much information the old man took in. To be honest, Mr. Danny didn't really work anymore. These days, he only showed up for about an hour each morning. His role was largely ceremonial. He mixed the yeast and puttered around the cooler for a few minutes. He gave Iggy the same baking instructions he always gave him, because in his mind Iggy was still a child who knew nothing and needed to be told all over again every day how to do things. Then he left, towed out the door by his son, and returned to the house on Lincoln Boulevard where the two of them had lived since the Johnson administration.

"Good morning, Mr. Danny. Good morning, Len," said Iggy.

"*Dzień dobry,*" said Mr. Danny.

Iggy looked in surprise at Len, who shrugged.

"He's been speaking Polish lately," he said. "And dreaming about his parents."

Iggy nodded. He knew what that meant; Mr. Danny's time was coming soon. He had often noticed that very old people mentally returned to their childhoods in the weeks and months before their deaths. Mr. Danny was probably remembering a time when you were far more likely to hear Polish than English on the streets of Buffalo.

"Dzień dobry," he said to Mr. Danny.

Len got the yeast from the cooler and set a mixing bowl on the counter in front of his father. Iggy headed for the front of house. He didn't need to see this ritual enacted yet again. Besides, he had work to do if they were going to serve any customers at all tonight.

"Iggy," said Len.

Iggy turned.

"Yeah?" he said.

"Thanks for letting him come back to work all this time," said Len.

Iggy shrugged. "Of course," he said.

"I know he hasn't actually been much help. It's probably the only thing kept him going," said Len. "It's been good for him. I appreciate it."

Iggy had the uncomfortable sense that Len was about to express an emotion, so he nodded quickly and went out front to examine the state of the seating area. As always, he immediately wished he hadn't.

The place had needed a makeover for twenty years. Yet again, the cleaning fairies had failed to show up and turn the place into a sparkling paradise, and Gordon Ramsay hadn't materialized with his teams of workmen to give it a complete makeover and turn the business around from the suicidal path it was on. No one besides Iggy knew that he had actually applied to be featured on Ramsay's show, *Kitchen Nightmares*, but had been turned down by the show's producers. Not even Gordon Ramsay could see the magic behind Polish food, apparently. Not the way Iggy could.

He stood with his hands on his hips and looked around at the chipped and greasy formica tabletops, bare of their plastic tablecloths for the moment; the grimy rug that should have been ripped up and thrown away in 1989; the plastic palms in the corners that had nothing to do with Poland, or with anything, really, but which he had adamantly refused to throw away; the mural of famous Polish-Americans that had been painted on the wall by someone with an art degree thirty years earlier, and which was now faded and half-covered by a coatrack, a mirror, the cash register, and a poster advertising a circus that had come to Warsaw in 2001.

At the far end of the room, there hung another picture. This one was a portrait in an old-fashioned oval frame covered with rounded glass. It was of a young woman, a beautiful woman—not in the sense of a delicate flower, but with a burgeoning femininity that hinted at an awesome, fulminating sea of energy and creativity just under the surface. It was his great-grandmother, Aniela, on her wedding day—the only such portrait of her that existed, taken on the only occasion she had ever worn such a fine dress, on one of the happiest days of her life. She was twenty-four years old in this portrait, but you did not see twenty-four-year-olds with that kind of quiet knowledge and exhaustion in their eyes anymore. Perhaps that was a good thing.

Iggy had not looked closely at this picture for a long time. He did so now, rediscovering it. It seemed to change every time he looked at it; or maybe it was he who had changed, and it merely reflected back a new part of himself. He stood there with his hands on his hips, remembering for a moment his great-grandmother's gnarled arthritic fists, the laughter she seemed able to summon only when children were in the room, her chocolate-chip cookies, the way she used to rub lard on her skin to keep it soft and white.

Iggy looked around to make sure he was alone.

"I'm sorry," he whispered to the portrait.

Then he went to the closet to get out the vacuum cleaner.

3. ELLIS ISLAND (JUNE 1908)

Their ship did not sink after all. It sailed grandly past the great statue of the Green Lady, she who held the torch of freedom in the air, to land at Ellis Island. The mood among the passengers from steerage, always chaotic, now became frenzied. People shouted at each other to be heard over the din, and that just made everything louder.

They disembarked into a great hall that was even larger than the ship. The dimensions of it left them speechless. Wonders of engineering such as this were built by God, who directed the hands of man. The place was filled with thousands of people. Maybe tens of thousands. Aniela and her sisters clung to their mother and to each other, terrified lest they be separated and never see one another again.

Uniformed staff members directed them to join a line of people that snaked into eternity. They waited in line for hours. They had nothing left to eat, and there was no water anywhere. It was hot in the hall. Chaos seemed to be the rule here, just as it had been aboard the ship. Babies and children cried, and sometimes their parents cried, too. Some people waited somberly, while others chattered nervously to their neighbors in their own languages, heedless of whether they were even understood.

The line moved so slowly that sometimes Aniela wondered if waiting was all there was to life in Ameryka. They still didn't even know if they would be allowed in. Throughout the journey this had been their fear, and for the months before that, before they even left home, they had wondered, too. If only there was some way to find out ahead of time, so that you didn't have to leave your entire life behind. It felt like gambling. It *was* gambling.

When it was finally their turn to speak to the customs agent, Jadwiga, who had graduated from the eighth form and was therefore the most educated, answered for all of them. She had the best handwriting, so she had already written their names on a piece of paper. The agent copied them into his ledger. Through a translator, an elderly woman in pince-nez glasses who stood next to him, she told him where they had come from, where they were going, and how much money they had with them.

They knew it was possible to get turned away if you showed any sign of disease or feeble-mindedness, so each woman made sure to stand up straight and look as healthy and alert as possible. *Not a sneeze or a sniffle,* Zofia had warned them on the ship. *Be serious. Don't smile like an idiot. Don't give them any reason to doubt us.*

Aniela felt herself growing light-headed again. All throughout the journey, everyone around them had constantly given voice to the same fear in a thousand different ways: *Will I get in*? There were many reasons why an immigrant might be turned away. It was entirely possible that one of them would be put on a boat and sent back home; and if one of them had to go, they would all go. This was what they had promised each other.

But Aniela had not meant it when she made that promise. If they were sent back, she had already decided, she would simply run out of the building, down to the rocky shore, and fling herself into the sea. She could not face the return trip, and there was no doubt in her mind that she would rather die than return to the country once known as Poland and which now couldn't even be found on a map.

She couldn't swim, so she knew the end would be quick.

But that hadn't happened. Instead came questions.

"Where are you going?"

"Buffalo."

"Who do you know there?"

"We know a Pan Gregor Stadnicki. He owns a hotel." This was a half-lie, but a carefully calculated one. There really was a man named Gregor Stadnicki, and Zofia had once known a woman who had met his aunt. The agent didn't need to know that Pan Stadnicki wouldn't know them if he tripped over them.

"Is he expecting you?"

"Yes." *It won't be a lie*, Jadwiga had argued. *He won't be surprised to see four more people from Poland show up asking for work.* Zofia had accepted this transgression as a necessity, but, she told Jadwiga, she would be confessing it to the first priest they found, as soon as possible.

"Is there no man traveling with you?"

Jadwiga fell silent, tongue-tied.

"Are you women traveling alone?" the inspector prodded.

"Yes."

"Why?"

"I'm sorry. I don't understand."

"Why is there no man with you?"

Jadwiga turned to Zofia, who remained stoic. For a fear-filled moment, Aniela wondered if Jadwiga was going to concoct another crazy story to explain their lack of a proper male chaperone. She was given to making up wild fables at a moment's notice. Normally she did this for her sisters' entertainment. But in this situation, it could get them into big trouble.

"Our father...had to stay behind," she said. "He is old. And our brothers stayed with him to work on the farm."

"We cannot let unescorted women into the country alone."

"W...what did he say?" Zofia asked the interpreter.

"It's for your own good. Women cannot be allowed to be on their own here. There are too many unscrupulous people waiting to take advantage of you."

Oh, my dear Father God, Aniela thought. *Over before it starts*. She began to feel dizzy.

"When you get through this line, you will find representatives of a Polish immigrant society there," the inspector continued. "Go straight to them and report yourselves as unescorted. They will assign a member of the train staff to chaperone you."

"Yes, sir," said Jadwiga.

To the others, she said, "He is letting us in."

All of them tried to control themselves. Zofia stepped forward, but Aniela grabbed her skirt and gave it a hard yank. She knew her mother had been about to bend and kiss the man's hand, the way one did to the priest or one of the noble family that had owned their village and the land they farmed. That would have been embarrassing beyond measure.

The inspector handed each of them a card.

"Don't lose these," he said through the interpreter. "These identify you as aliens. You'll need them when you apply for citizenship. You may pass."

Were they Americans now? They didn't even know. Dumbly, they did as they were told, clutching their cards as if the instructions for life itself were written upon them.

They were directed into another line. This one led toward a single man, very official-looking in a white coat, who scrutinized them as they walked toward him, one by one.

Apparently, they passed whatever test he was applying to them, for then they were ordered to turn right, where another medical man awaited. He also watched the women walk toward him, as if he could read every detail of their life in their gait and posture. When they stopped in front of him, he pulled back their eyelids and looked inside their mouths, as if they were horses. Then, through another translator, he ordered each of them to open her blouse.

"Why must we do this?" Zofia cried in horror.

The translator, a woman who spoke strange-sounding Polish, answered her. "They must check your skin to make sure you have no contagious diseases. Everyone must do it."

"But I don't know him! Is he even a doctor?"

"*Pani*, this is what you must do. Just show him you are healthy. He's not asking for his own pleasure, I assure you."

"Mother?" said Aniela fearfully.

"Show him," said Zofia, resignation in her voice.

All around them, lives were being changed in an instant, in the most dramatic fashion. Lone children cried for their parents. Parents frantically sought children who had been whisked away from them without notice, after showing signs of eye or lung disease. Aged parents who were denied entry bid farewell to their healthy adult children, knowing they would never see each other again but determined that this branch of the family would take root in the New World.

It was as if Ellis Island was a piece of cheesecloth, thought Aniela. You were squeezed unmercifully, and some part of you got through, while the rest was left behind to be discarded. She had thought that the ship was the most horrible place she'd ever been, but this place was worse.

Aniela opened her blouse and closed her eyes. She could feel the man's eyes upon her like the Devil's fingers. He was assessing her as if she was a farm animal. Well, it was not the first time a man had regarded her as nothing more than a beast of burden.

"You may cover yourselves again," the woman said.

Next, the four women were ordered to march down a corridor and turn to the right, where they found themselves in a separate, large hall. Here, under the watchful eyes of more government officials, they changed their money: *złoty* and rubles for American dollars. They had saved that money for years, and it was difficult to hand it over. When they received their strange new, green currency, Zofia counted it over and over. Aniela could tell by the way her lips worked that she was trying to do the sums in her head. Zofia had never been to school, and she struggled with larger numbers, though she would never admit it. Counting together, the women determined that it came to just over two hundred dollars. On one hand, it seemed like a fortune. On the other, it seemed like a pathetic and precarious foothold. When this money was gone, there was nothing else.

That was it. They were in Ameryka. But there were more steps to make: they must get to the train station, and then there was the train ride to Buffalo. They still had a long way to go.

Of this leg of the journey, Aniela remembered little. It was just another long voyage, fraught with unpredictability and dangers and too many strange new sights to take in. There was a time when a trip by train would have been enough excitement for the rest of her life. Now, after all they had been through, it was just one more detail in a crazy quilt of events. She had known traveling to Ameryka would change her, but she could not have imagined how greatly. She had become the kind of girl who thought nothing of a train journey of hundreds of miles.

And now, after all that, they were in their new home: a rooming house on Peter Street, in the neighborhood of Buffalo known as Black Rock.

Weeks went by, and time continued to speed up instead of slowing down again. The four of them shared a bedroom. The sourdough yeast, alive and bubbling in its crockery jar, sat off in a corner where no one could accidentally knock it over, wrapped in blankets to keep it safe. It was like a fifth guest in the room. As she lay in bed, trying to sleep despite the turmoil in her head, Aniela could smell the sourdough with her keen nose. It was about the only familiar thing in this strange new place, and she found its sharp tang comforting beyond measure.

They had found their house with the assistance of the immigrant society. Many Poles of all types had already come here to Buffalo to live. There were so many Poles, in fact, you could go about your business all day long and never hear a word of English.

Which suited Aniela just fine. Her only experience with a second language so far had been German, which she'd learned at school. This was certainly not by choice. If you spoke Polish, you were beaten. She herself had felt the sting of their Prussian teacher's belt on her hands numerous times.

She seemed powerless to stop the violence the German language conferred upon her. Whenever the teacher called on her, she froze. She could wring a chicken's neck, skin a rabbit, weed a garden, help deliver a baby, or wrangle a recalcitrant cow, but she couldn't think in German, not with that horrible, pasty-faced man screaming at her to hurry up and say the answer. Slovenly Poles, he called them, dirty pigs, filthy animals; they all deserved to be eradicated. Someday, he promised his class of terrified children, all Poles would either be Germanized or dead. In either case, the world would be a better place.

Small wonder she had left school before the age of twelve. She was never going to learn anything useful there anyway. A girl of her station didn't need an education. Her only purpose in life was to get married, produce children, and run a house, possibly a small farm. She had already mastered everything she would need to know by the time she got her first blood. There was practically nothing she couldn't do. Her mother was proud of her, and of all the girls. They would make fine wives and mothers.

But what Zofia didn't know was that Aniela planned on remaining unmarried and childless. In fact, she planned on having nothing to do with men whatsoever. The Prussian teacher had been only half right. It wasn't just Polish men who were pigs. It was all men, everywhere. This had been her experience with just about every man she'd ever met. She would have liked to have been proven wrong, but so far it hadn't happened. Her father was cruel to her mother. Her brothers were cruel to their sisters. Even the priest got so drunk on vodka sometimes that his hands seemed not to know what they were doing, and this was a man of God. All the girls in the village knew to stay far away from him when he was on one of his benders, or they might get invited back to his cottage for a private confession.

Aniela shook her head. She had to remember to leave these old thoughts behind. That priest, that teacher, her father, her brothers, hadn't followed her to Ameryka, after all. She was safe from them now. And maybe the men of Ameryka would be different.

Besides, there were new challenges to deal with. It was all well and good to speak Polish in the streets of Black Rock, but eventually this business of English would have to be dealt with, or she would never succeed here—not unless she wanted to be an ignorant washerwoman all her life.

It seemed that she was not destined to run a farmhouse after all. Instead they would live here, in Buffalo, one of the greatest cities on earth. She would become a city girl. That meant she would have to learn new skills. As yet, she didn't even know what those should be. But first and foremost, it meant learning English.

She had known English would be difficult, but she hadn't anticipated just *how* difficult. Maybe it would have been easier if she was forced to speak it in order to get by. But here in Buffalo, everyone was Polish: the baker, the butcher, the ragman, the iceman, the tinker, the sharpener, the undertaker, the dry grocer, the barber, the harness-maker, the midwives. There was even a Polish physician, for those who could afford him.

The family had chosen Buffalo for that very reason. They wanted to be among their own people. It was only natural. There were also many Poles in Chicago, but the journey there was much longer, and Zofia thought that city would be too big for them. Their village was home to only a few hundred souls; they were just country people, peasants, nothing more. Any further west, they would be among red Indians. If they headed south, alligators and malaria awaited.

Besides, all the work was here in the North. This was where the factories were. The great lake called Erie was crowded with ships loading and unloading goods from other parts of Ameryka, as well as from Europe and points even more distant. Thousands of men labored on the docks. Many thousands more had jobs at one of the steel plants or grain mills. Some of them were making as much as eighteen or twenty cents an hour. It was not as much as the non-Polish workers were paid, but still it was a sum unheard of in Poland. Plenty of Poles were sending money home to their families, and it was good money, too.

And Buffalo itself was as magnificent as a place you might read about in the Bible. The City of Light, they called it, because it had electric lights on the streets, powered by the mighty Niagara River. It was the first city in the world to achieve this miracle. How could water make light? It was an alchemical mystery. Not even the wise old women of her village would have known what to make of it.

Yet there was one of these lights on the street right outside their rooming house. It was a glass globe atop a tall pole, protected by an iron cage. Aniela often stared at it in the evenings, but she could discern no wick, no flame. It didn't even flicker. It burned with a steadiness and brightness that seemed magical.

This was the famous electricity, then. It was strange to her that she could not see the electricity itself—only the light it produced. What would Agnieszka think of that, if she were to describe it in a letter? How could she even explain it without sounding crazy?

But electricity was only one of the wonders Aniela had already learned to accept. Within a day of their arrival, she'd witnessed what looked like a wagon with a man sitting inside, moving along without any horses pulling it. She and her sisters had already learned to hide their astonishment at everything, because they didn't want to be laughed at for their ignorance. But she and Jadwiga couldn't help themselves this time; they stopped and stared as if they were seeing a two-headed calf.

At least they were not the only ones staring. Everyone looked. The horseless carriage made a horrible racket, and it put out clouds of smoke like the fires of hell were burning underneath it. The man who conducted it seemed to be enjoying the attention he attracted as he drove down the muddy street, swerving to avoid the largest piles of horse manure—though he made a point of looking straight ahead, pretending to be oblivious. Aniela and Jadwiga grabbed each other's hands. They had heard stories of these things, but they hadn't believed they would ever really see one. They stared after it even once it had passed.

"I want to ride in one of those one day," said Jadwiga.

"You wouldn't dare!" said Aniela, scandalized. "No decent woman would ever do such a thing."

"Women here do all kinds of things," Jadwiga told her. "They go all kinds of places. They do all sorts of things. They even smoke cigarettes sometimes."

"What would Mother say if you rode in one of those?"

"Who cares?" Jadwiga snorted. "She would never even know. Unless someone told on me." She cast a warning glare at her younger sister.

Aniela felt that things were changing far too fast. Jadwiga was already talking like their life in Poland was a thousand years in the past. It felt like that to her, too, but she seemed to be taking to the changes less readily than her more adventurous sister. She would never say she was homesick; that was not the right way to describe it. But all the same, nothing here was familiar. The smell of the sourdough and the sound of Polish being spoken on the streets were not enough to trick her into believing she belonged here.

Yet Ameryka's promises were beginning to unfold, too. Just weeks after their arrival, Aniela had a book.

It was the first book she'd ever had all to herself. That alone made it precious. A nice woman at Assumption of the Blessed Virgin Mary, the church on the corner of Peter and Amherst, had given it to her. It was called *English for New Americans*. It had some phrases in Polish, then the corresponding phrase in English. She practiced with her sisters: *Hello, how are you today? I would like to buy some butter. The weather is very fine.*

Some English words, like *house, mother, father,* or *bread* were easy, because they sounded a great deal like their German versions.

Other things about English made no sense to her, though. In particular, the dreaded letters *-ough* made her want to scream in frustration. Tough, through, bough, though…would there never be enough? The lady at the church offered lessons; they were held one evening a week in the Sunday school class-room, and they were always full of students of all ages. She would write things on the slate chalkboard like:

When he saw the tear in the curtain, a tear ran down his cheek.
When you record something, you make a record of it.
If you are Polish, polish your shoes.

"But the words are the same!" her students would howl. "How can you know when to say REC-ord and when to say re-CORD?"

The lady would smile and laugh, because she understood their frustration. She had been born here in Ameryka, but her parents were Polish, and she spoke both languages fluently. She tried to explain it to them. Many were able to grasp the difference. But to Aniela, who sometimes felt as if her head had not stopped spinning from the moment she got on that cursed ship, it was just too much.

Well, she hadn't come here to go to school; she had come here to work and to get ahead in life. That was what mattered, wasn't it?

In fact, just weeks after their arrival, she already had a job.

Polish workers, both men and women, were much in demand throughout Buffalo. They had reputations as honest and hard-working people. Though they had already been in the city for forty or fifty years, and there were upwards of seventy thousand of them in this city full of immigrants, every Pole seemed mindful that it wouldn't take much to turn the tide of public opinion against them. The man who seven years earlier had shot the American president, McKinley, was a Buffalo Pole. The community was still reeling from the effects of that horrible incident, which had happened right here, in this city. Everyone felt it brought shame upon them, and they encouraged each other to make sure their comportment was above reproach at all times. If Poles started to get a reputation for criminal behavior, that would only make it harder for all of them.

So Aniela wasted no time finding work. Within days, she had a job doing laundry and housework at the home of a doctor in downtown Buffalo. It meant getting up early in the morning, well before sunrise, and walking to Niagara Street, then taking a streetcar on an endless ride into the city.

The directions were written out for her by Pani Grzyb, the lady who taught English classes. Even so, that first journey, which cost an entire nickel, was one of the most frightening experiences of Aniela's life. It was nearly as momentous as her Atlantic crossing.

Firstly, like the streetlight outside their rooming house, the streetcar was powered by electricity; it was a giant wagon that had no horses pulling it, and yet it moved as fast as the carriage belonging to the szlachcianka. She could only imagine what the priest back home would have said. Likely he would have considered this a form of witchcraft. She almost laughed as she imagined the expression on his alcohol-reddened face, watching the streetcar pass by. Maybe it would splash him with mud and manure. That would be fitting, she thought.

Secondly, Buffalo had so many buildings that they blocked the sun, and they all looked the same to her. She knew the names of a hundred different trees; she could identify dozens of different breeds of cows, goats, and chickens; she could tell just by looking at a horse who in the village owned it, how old it was, and what it was used for. But she could not for the life of her tell these buildings apart. Not yet. Maybe someday.

Thirdly, she had not yet learned the street names, nor could she read very well, so she had to look at the shape of the words on the paper and compare them to the shape of the words on the signs. This was very difficult. On her first day, she was terrified that she would be late for work and get fired before she'd even started. If word got out that she was lazy and irresponsible, she imagined it would be no time at all before the authorities would decide Ameryka didn't need types like her, and she would be put on the next ship back to Poland. They had already been warned by the ladies at the immigrant society: until you became a citizen, you had to watch your step very carefully, or you would get sent back. It didn't happen often, but it did happen.

This thought was enough to keep all four of them in a state of perpetual nervousness. They did nothing without double-checking with the immigrant society first, and sometimes even with the priest at the church on the corner, Assumption of the Blessed Virgin Mary: Would this be all right? Was that all right? Should they do this, or not do that? Their lives were governed by a fear of consequences for breaking laws they didn't fully understand. But that, too, was nothing new. In fact, compared to life under the Prussians, it was like being on holiday. At least they didn't have to worry about being beaten in the street for nothing.

Worst of all about this streetcar was that Aniela worried what people would think of her, roaming the city on her own like this. Decent women did not wander around like sheep without a shepherd. Being alone made her a prime target for any lecherous wolf with a bellyful of beer and a wandering eye. Aniela was no weakling; far from it, in fact. She knew that she was as strong as any of her brothers, and stronger than many of the boys in the village—though as a girl you had to be careful to hide that fact, lest you offend their delicate egos. And she knew from experience that a smart blow with the ridge of her hand to the upper lip, or the side of the neck, would usually discourage even the most amorous of wolves.

But she preferred to avoid that entire scenario altogether. So she sat right behind the streetcar driver, clutching her bag and trying to accomplish the impossible task of seeing absolutely everything while looking demurely at the floor.

The strange thing about Ameryka was that you couldn't tell just by looking at someone what part of the world they came from. In Poland, it was easy to tell by someone's style of dress what group they belonged to: Polish, Prussian, Ruthenian, Gypsy, Slovak, and Jew were the most common, and occasionally, in places like Poznań, you might see Hungarians, Slovenians, Russians, Austrians, and others as well. But here, the men wore pants with suspenders, shirts, jackets, and hats of all descriptions; the women wore dresses that reached to their ankles, and lace-up boots or shoes. There seemed to be no such thing as tradition, unless not having a national costume was the new tradition. It was as if people were trying to blend in with each other on purpose.

That made sense. They were all Americans now, Aniela reasoned. They were supposed to melt together, like the ingredients in a stew.

But she didn't feel like an American. She still just felt like herself. It was hard for her to imagine, as the streetcar worked its way down Niagara Street, with the river rushing by on the right and Canada so close you could throw a rock into it, that she would ever be anything more than a Polish village girl far from home.

The streetcar's bell dinged, and she looked up to see yet another astonishing thing. There, waiting to cross the street, was a man, a woman, and two children—all four of them with black skin.

Black skin! Her first thought was that they must have been horribly burned somehow. But they didn't appear to be in pain.

Then she realized: these were Africans. Somewhere far away was a whole nation of people who looked like this. She had heard of these people. But she could never have imagined what it would be like to see one up close.

What would it be like to actually *be* one of them? she wondered. Were they Christian people? They must be, for God had created them, too, hadn't He? But if God created everything and everyone, could He even create people who didn't believe in Him?

The world was so overwhelmingly big that it hurt to think about it. She clutched her bag closer and stared straight ahead at the driver's neck. She had seen enough memorable sights to last her for the rest of her life, yet she was not even seventeen years old.

4. KENMORE (SEPTEMBER 2015)

Angela's opened for dinner at 5:00 p.m. At 4:37, which was thirty-seven minutes late, Yogi, Iggy's morally questionable niece, appeared to start her shift waiting tables.

Iggy would always have a soft spot for Yogi, no matter how egregious her sins. It was that soft spot that had prevented him from firing her, despite the fact she deserved it, many times over. When she was tiny, she used to call him Unka Icky, which had melted his heart, even though "Icky" was one of numerous insults other children had flung at him when he was small. She would lead him around the restaurant by one finger, showing him obvious items as though they were the most fascinating things in the world. He and Silvestra had never had children of their own, so he had allowed Yogi into that part of his heart that would normally have been reserved for a daughter.

Now, she was a busty twenty-three-year-old with a large, white belly, what seemed to be three simultaneous hairstyles, and a fondness for crop-tops and tight jeans. Rolls of fat around her middle overhung her pants in plain sight of everyone, while the situation up top left practically nothing to the imagination. To say that she was an embarrassment was certainly to understate the matter.

Iggy secretly hated each of Yogi's eleven visible tattoos, but his least favorite was the one on her left shoulder blade, which was of some kind of Japanese cartoon character with big eyes and huge breasts. This character was plunging a samurai sword through a row of three men. One wore a business suit, one wore a military uniform, and one wore the frock of a Catholic priest. The cartoon character was skewering these men on her sword like cocktail onions. Yogi was not a huge fan of something she called The Patriarchy. As far as Iggy could tell, The Patriarchy seemed to mean any man who had authority over her. That was what the three men in the image symbolized, he guessed.

"You're late," he said to Yogi.

"So?" said Yogi. "Literally no one is coming anyway." She looked as if she might keel over and die from ennui as she headed for the silverware section.

"Someone might," Iggy said.

"You always say that."

"Because it's true. You never know who is going to walk in the door. You have to be ready."

"I literally cannot wait for this place to close," said Yogi, "so I can get on with my life."

She picked up a napkin and started half-heartedly polishing the butter knives, tossing them back in the silverware tray when she was done. "No one is going to show up," she added, as Iggy opened the doors to the kitchen. "We might as well close early."

"You have to be ready," Iggy said. "There are a lot of hungry people in the world," he added.

He headed back to the dishwashing area, where Jesús, who hailed originally from the city of Chihuahua, Mexico, was already at his station, waiting for dishes that would probably never come. Jesús was in his early thirties, and he had a wife and three children at home. During his endless cell phone conversations in the parking lot, which took place during his marathon cigarette breaks, he frequently referred to the Podbielskis as *los Polacos*. This was about the only Spanish that Iggy understood. At the moment, Jesús was reading a comic book.

"Not smoking, I see," Iggy greeted him. "Everything all right?"

Jesús smirked at him. "You find me a new job yet?"

"Have a little faith," said Iggy.

Jesús rattled off something in Spanish, a language that Iggy had never even begun to learn. English was enough for him; he was privately embarrassed about the fact that he didn't even understand more than ten or twenty words of Polish.

"What's that mumbo-jumbo mean?" he asked.

"It mean, like, you should have faith in God, but you should also make good plans."

"That's what my grandmother used to say," said Iggy.

"That's what *my* grandmother say," Jesús said, grinning at him with his gold-rimmed teeth.

"Maybe our grandmothers should have been drinking buddies," Iggy said.

"My grandmother could drink your grandmother over the table," said Jesai.

"Under the table."

"Whatevers."

"Well, then," Iggy said, and because this situation seemed to be well in hand, he headed next into the kitchen area.

This was the territory of Bronisława "Brownie" Blankenship, Iggy's fifty-year-old cousin, whose tenure as chef coincided rather neatly with the decline of Angela's, though Iggy didn't blame her for that. Her cooking was fine. Not great, but perfectly adequate. Brownie had been to cooking school, and she could turn out the old standards that the blue-haired set was still fond of.

The problem wasn't the quality of the food. The problem, in her eyes, was that most people just didn't want Polish any more. It was too old-fashioned, Brownie was always telling Iggy: too heavy, too starchy. There was a reason you didn't see any thin Polish women around here. And if a Polish man was thin, it was because he subsisted on a diet of liquid potatoes, which was what Brownie called vodka.

"We need to go *artisanal* if we're going to survive," she had told Iggy just the month before. "Home-smoked sausages, like they used to make. And get back to baking. Pickling. Preserving. Traditional Polish values. Start selling that stuff."

"Artisanal is not what Angela's is about," Iggy had said.

"Artisanal is where your value-added is," Brownie said.

"Value-added? What is value-added? Angela's started out as a bakery. It makes no sense to go back to being a bakery.

That would be moving backwards." For despite all evidence to the contrary, Iggy prided himself on being a forward-looking man.

"You," said Brownie, "are not listening to one goddamn word I'm saying. I'm not saying don't do the restaurant. I'm saying do this *with* the restaurant. People really go for that stuff these days. And change the food."

"Change the *food*? Change it to what? Italian?"

"Nouveau Polonaise," said Brownie.

Iggy had nearly choked on his Diet Coke, which was what he had become addicted to after he gave up liquid potatoes himself, about fifteen years earlier.

"What language is that? French?"

"Good guess," said Brownie. "It means New Polish."

"New Polish."

"We need to reimagine the entire menu. Re-present it. Re-package it. Re-design it. What we need is a dose of creativity here."

"New Polish," said Iggy, "will never fly in this town."

"Well, look how well Old Polish is flying," said Brownie, and to prove her point she picked up an unsauced *galumpki* and threw it at the wall. There it stuck like a glob of C-4 explosive, just waiting to be detonated.

They both stood there and stared at it for a while. Then Iggy sighed and walked away.

That was the last time Iggy and Brownie had had a conversation. Since then, they had mostly just nodded at each other, speaking only enough to make sure that the menu for the evening was planned and the ordering had been done.

There were so few portions being prepared these days that Iggy didn't need to check in with the staff at all. The fact was, they were all correct. No one was going to come in for dinner tonight. Especially not with that new graffiti on the wall outside, and the broken sign. The place looked vacant. At the last family meeting, it had been decided to put the land up for sale and to stop investing in the property or the business.

Angela's, or some variation of it, had sustained his family for the last four generations, and Iggy had long hoped it would sustain them for another four. But it looked like this was the end. It was time to put it down, like a horse with four broken legs.

From five o'clock to eight o'clock, the staff waited for diners to show up. Jesús smoked and made cell phone calls. Yogi snuck shots of liquid potatoes from the bar. Brownie leaned over the gleaming and spotless prep table in the kitchen, frowning at her laptop. Iggy stood by the cash register, ready to greet anyone who might walk in the door, a smile plastered on his face. He watched the traffic go by on Delaware Avenue and wondered if anyone in those cars had ever been into his restaurant before, and if so, why they had stopped coming. He would really like it if someone would just hand him an answer to all his questions right now. He still had boundless energy. He would still bend over backwards to do what needed to be done. He just didn't know what that was.

At eight o'clock, having served no one, he closed the restaurant for the evening, and they all went home.

"Thanks, everyone, for a really great night," said Iggy. It was what he always said at the end of the day. But nobody answered him. He doubted whether they'd even heard a word he said.

5. BLACK ROCK (AUGUST 1909)

Aniela worked. Jadwiga worked. Catharina worked. Zofia worked. All of them had found the same kind of employment: housecleaning, laundering, sometimes cooking, in the homes of wealthy families. They were servants, yet they were their own masters. They were not beaten. No one cursed at them or called them Polish bitches. They were paid wages that in Poland would have been a fortune. It was a strange twist on an old dynamic: they were still at the bottom rung, but they felt wealthy.

The women had always been used to working all day long, from sunup to sundown, with little respite except on Sunday, when they only had to milk the cows and goats, gather any eggs, feed the animals, walk to church, walk back from church, and prepare meals for the family. That was their day off. The other six days, they completed the endless round of chores that made up life on a farm. It never even would have occurred to them to complain, because work was what a good life consisted of. They had no reason to hope for anything more. Had it not been for the merciless Prussians crushing them under their shiny black leather boots, they might have been content to live like that forever. There was no shame in it, and there was a great deal of satisfaction. But the Prussians had been running the show for over 150 years, and there was no reason to believe that was ever going to change.

Now, each of them worked inside, at different houses, for different wealthy families. They met up again in the evenings, back at the rooming house on Peter Street. There they ate dinner and compared their experiences.

"I saw more people with black skin today," Aniela said.

"At my house there is a lady with black skin who works there," Catharina said. "She takes care of their children. Sometimes I am *this close* to her." She held up her hands to indicate proximity. "And do you know what? She is a Christian."

"A…Christian? But how?" Aniela said.

Catharina shrugged.

"God made everything on the earth and everyone in it," said Zofia.

Aniela considered this fact. If an African person could be a Christian, then God was even more powerful than she had known. And it meant that they were more like her than she had even realized. What a world it was.

"At *my* house, they have a machine that washes the clothes all by itself," Jadwiga said casually.

By now, Aniela had become almost inured to such shocking statements. If entire wagonloads of people could move down the street without horses pulling them, if light could be made from water, then it was certainly possible for clothing to wash itself. It wouldn't have surprised her a bit to look out the window and see ladies' dresses and men's suits taking themselves for a walk, with no people inside them. That was the kind of thing you came to expect in Ameryka.

Last week, another kind of machine had passed by—not on the street, but overhead, in the middle of the air, like a bird. It was called an aeroplane. The entire city of Buffalo had turned out to see it. Aniela was told that there was a man inside it, flying along as naturally as if he was riding a horse. You could even see his head as the aeroplane dipped and dove. Never before in the history of the world had so many amazing inventions come into being. And she was right in the middle of it.

She couldn't bear to hear any more about washing machines. Things were moving too fast, and she needed time to catch up.

But Zofia demanded to know what Jadwiga was talking about. So Jadwiga demonstrated, pretending the machine stood before her.

"It looks like a laundry tub on legs," she said. "You put the water in from a bucket like normal, and you heat it from below with the flame from a gas pipe, like we have coming out of the wall. You put the soap in. Then you just turn it on."

"What do you mean, 'turn it on'?" Zofia asked.

"It runs on electricity, Mother," said Jadwiga. "You don't have to do anything. You move a little lever with your finger, and the beaters move up and down and side to side. You have to be careful not to put in too much water, or it spills."

"I don't understand," said Zofia, but she also didn't seem to really want to understand; she appeared too tired to absorb further explanation.

"And what do you do, while these clothes are washing themselves?" Catharina sneered.

Jadwiga shrugged. "I wait," she said. "I relax. I read the newspaper in English."

"Oh ho! Little Miss Szlachcianka," said Catharina.

"She *smokes*," Aniela said contemptuously.

"I should hope not!" Zofia said.

"How would Aniela know what I do? She's not even there," Jadwiga said. Her eyes threatened her sister with murder. "She's just jealous because *her* employers aren't rich enough to own an electric washing machine, and she still has to do it with her hands."

Aniela was in no mood for this game. The rivalry that sometimes existed between the sisters had survived the transatlantic journey unscathed. She decided to strike back, childish though it may be. "That's not all, Mother. She told me she's going to ride in an automobile with a man someday!" Aniela cried.

Zofia drew back in horror, as if the Devil had slapped her across the mouth with his tail. Then she crossed herself and kissed her fingertips.

"That's enough!" she snapped. "The three of you shut your mouths and listen to me."

The girls fell silent. They could tell whatever was coming was about to be big.

"First of all, keep your voices down. I don't want the whole house listening in on our problems.

"Second of all, no good can come from any of this modern nonsense. What kind of woman stands by and lets a machine do her work for her? It's not healthy. Idle hands do the Devil's work."

"Well, then, I'll just tell the MacMillans they have to return their washing machine because my mother doesn't approve," said Jadwiga, sullen.

"And thirdly," said Zofia, ignoring this insolence, "girls, it breaks my heart to see how this new life is already changing us. Nothing here makes any sense. Life is so strange that it seems like God has forsaken this country, if He had ever been here at all. There are no values. No morals. Everyone just does whatever he wants. This is no way for people to live. I just don't want to see you become the kind of women who...," she searched for words to adequately express the despair she felt, "...who ride in automobiles with men," she finished.

"We're not going back, are we?" asked Catharina, who was the youngest, and who, at fifteen, sometimes still cried herself to sleep at night when she thought no one could hear.

"No, we're not going back," said Zofia. She shuddered. "But I want all three of you to promise me you won't forget who you are."

Aniela wanted to say: *But who are we? The Prussians took our country off the map and took our language out of the schools. We're thousands of miles from home, and yet we have no home. We are not Poles. We are not Americans. So who are we?*

But instead she said, "*Tak, Ma.*"

"Tak, Ma," said Catharina.

"Okay, Ma," said Jadwiga.

"*Okay*? What is this *okay*?" Zofia said.

"It's Amerykańska slang," said Aniela. "It means she agrees."

Zofia closed her eyes and shook her head. The girls were expecting another salvo from her, but she said nothing further. She retreated to the bed the four of them shared, her rosary in her hands, her lips moving silently as she worked the beads.

Aniela thought that her mother had been looking more tired than usual, ever since they left Poland. She'd never known much about her private thoughts. Up until this moment, if someone had asked her, she would probably have answered that Zofia didn't have any private thoughts at all. She existed only for her family. She could see now that that was wrong. In a moment of insight, she realized that her mother was really no different than she, just a fifty-year-old version of herself—if she was lucky enough to live that long. It had been easier for the girls to make this move. After all, the three of them were young enough to adapt to anything.

But Zofia had already lived most of her life. At an age when the other women of the village could look forward to spending their final years among their friends and family, with grandchildren and perhaps great-grandchildren tumbling about their feet, and being laid to rest when their time came in the same cemetery as generations of their ancestors, instead Zofia could only look forward to an old age in a strange land, where they knew no one—and a cold, lonely eternity in a cemetery full of strangers.

Aniela knew, too, that other Poles in Black Rock wondered about them. It was normal for the men of a family to come ahead to Ameryka, to work and earn and save, and to send for their families when they had become established. But no one had ever heard of a mother and her daughters coming by themselves, with no men at all, nor even any mention of when they might be coming.

Nobody asked questions. People were too polite for that. But Aniela knew that everyone was curious, and she knew they would be shocked if they could read her mind: not only did they *not* long for their father and brothers to join them, as most immigrants did…such a thing was their greatest fear.

That first Friday after they had all begun working, the four of them opened their pay envelopes and put their money in a pile on the bed. Each of the women was making about ten cents an hour. Their wages ranged between five to six dollars per week apiece, for a total of twenty-two dollars.

Of their original two hundred dollars, which had taken so many years to save, they had paid about twenty for their train tickets to Buffalo. They had given another twenty to the landlady, which would allow them to stay in their rented room for two months. They had spent yet another twenty or so on the necessities of life. There had been other fees here and there. It seemed every time they turned around someone else was trying to squeeze a few drops of blood from them. They had scarcely a hundred dollars left.

However, already they had earned more in a week than they could have earned in months at home. Yes, things were more expensive here, but they seemed to be prospering. If things continued like this, then maybe Ameryka really would turn out to be the Promised Land for them. Soon they hoped to have enough for a payment on a house of their own. You could do that here in Ameryka—put down a little money on a house with a promise to pay the rest, and then you could say it was yours. It was called a *mortgage*. All over the city, other Poles were doing the same thing.

Not only that, but you could also rent out part of your house to other families. You could earn money with your house before it was even completely yours.

To get ahead, you had to save your money, work hard, and sacrifice comforts. This was the great American dream they had heard so much about. And they were each determined to grab as much of it as they could.

Each of them ate as little as possible: nothing more than cold *kasha* for breakfast, a sausage bun at dinnertime, and pierogies stuffed with cheese or *gołąbki* filled with rice for supper. Maybe some *kapusta* with *kluski*, if the weather was cold and they were feeling homesick. There was nowhere in the rooming house for them to cook, so they had to buy their food prepared every day, which was expensive. The sooner they had their own kitchen, the better.

Aniela had decided to save even more money by making the long walk to work instead of spending ten cents on a streetcar every day. It took her an hour each way, but it allowed her to save an extra sixty cents per week. Never in her life had she earned this kind of money. She could feel excitement rising deep within her whenever she thought about the future. That in itself was a whole new experience. No one in her family had ever had much reason to hope for anything better or different before. The hated Prussians had ruled them for generations now, and before then life had not been much easier, according to the stories she heard.

But that was the old country. The cord had been cut. She forced herself to stop looking backward, and to look ahead.

They were lucky to have a whole room all to themselves. Other rooms in the same house were overflowing with people. All night long you could hear them tramping back and forth, talking, singing drunkenly, fighting, crying. It was like a whole village crammed into one building. It was the same all over Buffalo, they knew. There were six or eight Polish families crammed into houses that were only meant for one or two. There was no shortage of work, but there was a big shortage of cheap housing.

For many years, a man named Bork had built houses and made them available to Polish immigrants for small down payments. Poles who in the old country could never have dreamed of owning a home now found themselves in possession of a house that no one could take away from them, unless they failed to make their payments—which none of them ever did. They would rather have died. Many of these houses even had a second storey that could be let out to another family, bringing in rental income for the owners. Thousands of Poles wrote home, telling family and friends that they too could become homeowners in Ameryka.

The result was a flood of Polaks. Almost one in every five people in Buffalo was from some part of Poland these days. They could not build houses fast enough to keep up with the demand.

With four of them working and saving, it would not be long before they had enough put by to make a down payment on a house of their own, should they find one. Ideally, it would have a second storey that they could rent out to another family. Then they, too, would become landlords.

Zofia was entrusted with keeping their money safe. She wrapped it up in a small black purse, which she kept stored in her bosom.

Aniela had to laugh. That money was probably safer there than it would have been in the Kaiser's palace. Even the inspector at Ellis Island would not have dared to reach in there.

After they finished counting the money, and with another minor squabble over nothing thrown in for good measure, Aniela and the others readied themselves for bed. As she drifted off to an exhausted sleep, she could smell the sourdough mixture bubbling away in the corner.

Late in the night, her mother got up to feed it, dropping a small piece of bread crust and a bit of water in. She even muttered something quietly to it, and though Aniela couldn't be sure, it sounded something like, *Grow, grow, and feed us all.*

6. KENMORE (SEPTEMBER 2015)

Family meeting.

How Iggy hated those words. They reminded him of the family meetings of his childhood. These were infrequent but highly stressful events, occurring only when there was bad news to deliver, or whenever his Baby Boomer parents felt there was a lack of drama in their lives. Big Stosh could go for ages without speaking to any of them, wrapped up as he was in running the restaurant. Then, suddenly, he would try to cram six months' worth of fathering into an hour or so. The family was falling apart, he would declare; they did not spend enough time together, they did not respect him as a father. His mother, not to be outdone, would manage to find some long-buried issue to get upset about at the same time, and so it would go until the entire family was shouting and in tears. Iggy would attend because he was forced to attend, but he would simply tune out and wish that he were somewhere else. He got very good at that.

In those days, he'd wanted nothing to do with the restaurant. As a child, he'd been stashed behind the cash register, observing the plump calves of the waitresses as they rang up checks, absorbing the ways of Podbielski-style customer service. When he was a little older, he'd been allowed to put on an apron and work in the kitchen. He would help mix the mashed potatoes, or he would be given his own dough ball by Mr. Danny to play with. He still remembered how proud he'd been when he managed to make something that Mr. Danny hadn't promptly spit out in the garbage upon tasting.

In those days, the restaurant was a warm, comforting, lively place, one of the cultural centers of Polonia in Buffalo. For many families, Angela's was the place you went to celebrate anything of any importance: a christening, a first Communion, a wedding, a funeral. There was scarcely a weekend when it wasn't booked for some kind of function. In the early 1990s, it had also been the scene of four massive annual parties, the likes of which had rarely been seen in those parts. In each of those years, the Buffalo Bills had made it all the way to the Super Bowl, and each time the people of the city had rejoiced in much the same way the ancient Israelites must have partied when they finally stumbled into the Promised Land.

Every Pole of Black Rock, whether they had been born in this country or the old, possessed a long list of tragedies that had been tattooed onto his very DNA, and which he mourned by emitting a constant, low-frequency sorrow. This was comprised of the effective expulsion of his people from their native land; the German slaughter of the Poles during the war; the Communist takeover following the war; and the four consecutive Super Bowl losses of the Buffalo Bills, from 1991 to 1994. Iggy could barely bring himself to think about those heartbreaking years, which had seemed so full of hope—1991, in particular, had seemed almost too good to bear, with the Berlin Wall having crumbled into dust and the Bills headed into the championship with an average of 26.75 points per game, the best in the league.

He shook his head to clear it. Life was painful enough without digging into old wounds.

When he turned fourteen, he remembered, he'd been stationed out front as a busboy. When he was sixteen, still a couple years shy of the legal age for serving alcohol but who was counting, he was allowed to wait tables. He learned how to take an order for a table of six without writing anything down, how to carry a tray of drinks without spilling a drop, how to calm the rare disgruntled customer, how to remember names from one year to the next, how to flatter the women, how to cater to the men, how to indulge the children.

People came to Angela's not just for the food, he discovered, but for the experience. If he had to be honest, he would have to say that the food was never anything more than reliable. It was not gourmet cooking. No, they came to feel happy, to feel wanted, to feel appreciated; also, he discovered, a lot of them wanted to feel like they had actually been to a little piece of Poland. Never mind that he himself had never been to Poland, that he barely spoke a word of the language, that he wouldn't know Poland if it walked up and punched him in the nose. He learned to play it up. He repeated stories he'd heard other people tell about the old days. He explained the food. He smiled even when he didn't feel like smiling. And people kept coming back.

Maybe he was a little too good at it. He was always in demand. Even when he was a teenager, evenings and weekends were taken up by work. He had no life outside the restaurant. He could not escape. Then he'd come to hate the place with a passion. Naturally, this brought out feelings of guilt. It had been drummed into his head how lucky they were to have a family business in the first place. They could have been poor or homeless, or worse yet they could have been back in Poland, shriveling under the Communists. Or they could have been dead, of course. That was another lesson that was drummed into his head: no matter how shitty things got, they could always get worse, so shut your pie-hole and get back to work. Back then he hadn't felt lucky. He felt like a prisoner whose only crime had been to be born to the wrong people.

This was when Iggy learned to live a secret, invisible fantasy life. When he was a teenager, he had wanted more than anything to be a rock star. And his fantasies would become particularly acute during family meetings.

He noted with irony that even at the age of forty-five, this tendency in him had not gone away. In fact, it was as strong as ever.

He stood before his family now, dozens of them, and as he waited for them to shut their pie-holes and pay attention to him, he wondered what his life would have been like had he followed his ambition and moved to L.A. to become a rock star. He'd probably be a heroin addict, he thought.

Iggy's parents were not physically in the room, but nevertheless he could feel them looming behind him, where they were displayed prominently on a fifty-inch flat-screen TV that he had set up on one of the tables in the dining room of the restaurant. Physically, they were in Florida, which was about a thousand miles too close for his liking. He would have preferred them somewhere around the equator, or possibly Mars. But because they were shareholders, they were allowed to participate in any meeting that related to the future of Angela's. This meant that according to the rules of the corporation, Iggy couldn't hold a family meeting without them.

He took comfort in the fact that he could at least mute them. That was an innovation that had come many years too late. He caressed the mute button on the remote now with his thumb, his back to the webcam that allowed his parents to see everyone in the room.

He looked around at them all, seated before him now: his two aunts and his uncle, all of them over the age of seventy; his younger brother, Harry, a medical equipment salesman; his sister, Veronica, who could best be described as a professional divorcée, and who was Yogi's mother; his cousins, nine of them, ranging in age from twenty-five to fifty or so, most of whom had never lifted a finger at the restaurant before but all of whom were no doubt hoping to profit from the sale of the place; Harry's daughters, aged twelve and fifteen, whom his brother had dragged here under threat of permanent revocation of the password to their home Wi-Fi network; Brownie and her "friend," Linda, a woman with a brush cut and a smug expression that Iggy was sure had gotten smugger since gay marriage had been ruled constitutional in recent weeks;

and several of his cousins' children, all of them under the age of fifteen. Even Whitey Lubek, his weird middle-aged cousin with the strange hairs growing out of his face, had come. That was an event. Everyone knew that Whitey was one of the smartest people who'd ever lived, but he rarely spoke to anyone, and he almost never left his house. It was said of him that he had two PhDs in subjects no one else understood, that he had written a number of books no one ever read, and he knew the entire history of Poland by memory. Actually, he lived with his mother and did not know how to do his own laundry. What a genius.

Silvestra herself was not there. Iggy wasn't surprised. She had no more stomach for these family meetings than did Iggy. She hardly set foot in the place at all anymore. They had met while she was working there as a waitress, when she and Iggy were both about twenty. They had great plans, and life had seemed very exciting, but as work took over his life, and they found it difficult for her to get pregnant, things had become rather drab, and they had drifted apart. Iggy did not even notice her absence; it would have been surprising if she'd been there.

Iggy privately marveled, as he always did, at the sheer number of people who had sprung from a single point on the family tree. There were at least thirty people in the room, and nearly all of them were here because of one person: Aniela.

Yet despite their shared origins, Iggy had never felt much in common with his family. Sometimes he felt like he'd come from a different planet. He'd ended up in charge of the restaurant because he was the one who had devoted the most time to it; his father, Big Stosh, had run it throughout the late '70s and '80s and well into the '90s, handing it over to Iggy just when numbers began to tank and everyone else developed a sudden disinterest in the place. He'd spent the last fifteen years trying to keep standards as high as he remembered them from his childhood, though to be honest he wasn't sure whether they had actually ever been that high or if he was just remembering it through the rose-colored lenses of memory.

Iggy had hoped to reach out to new markets. He had plans for expansion. He could see himself as the owner of not one but many restaurants, like Gordon Ramsay. Gordon Ramsay didn't let anyone push him around; he always said exactly what was on his mind, and people respected him for it.

But the old Polaks were all dying off by then, and this latest generation was thoroughly Americanized. To them, Polish culture was something only old people talked about, and it bore not the slightest relevance to their lives. They were just American people with Polish last names. You could not sustain a restaurant when the only time people came to eat at your place was at Christmas or Easter, and then only out of a sense of tradition. Iggy knew full well what tradition was: it was duty dressed up in church clothes. Some people liked traditions, but then some people liked being tied up and whipped, too.

Jesus, what the hell was wrong with him, thinking that way? He needed to focus.

He picked up a water glass and dinged it with the blade of a butter knife. The glass, a cheapo product that was made in China and which he had bought at Costco, promptly cracked. He shoved it behind his back, hoping no one had noticed and forgetting about the webcam that was on top of the TV set. Everyone fell silent.

"Way to go," said his father from behind him. "How much did that glass cost?"

"Iggy, *move*, I can't see," said his mother from the television.

Iggy gritted his teeth and stepped two paces to the left.

"All right," he said. "Everyone, I have an announcement."

They all sat and stared at him, waiting.

"Someone wants to buy the place," he said.

He waited for the applause to die down. For everyone else in the room, this was great news. So why did it feel like a knife to his heart?

"Who is it?" several people asked.

"I don't know. They want to remain anonymous," Iggy said. "They're buying through the bank."

"How much?"

"They lowballed a little," said Iggy, and he mentioned a figure. There was more applause, not as enthusiastic this time, but still buoyant.

"So, we need to take a vote," said Iggy.

"What's to vote on?" asked Brownie. "This is the thing we've been hoping for."

"On whether we accept their offer or not," Iggy said.

"Of course we accept their offer," said his father through the television behind him. "Are you crazy? This is the answer to our prayers."

"It's not too late to turn things around," Iggy continued, surreptitiously hitting the mute button on the remote. "I called everyone here so we could talk about it one last time."

"How many times do we have to talk about it one last time?" said one of his cousins, Jersey, whose birth name was actually Jerzy. "Haven't we already said nine thousand times we want to sell the place?"

"Yeah," said Harry. "Jesus, Iggy, I should be out making sales calls right now."

"Angela's Restaurant will cease to exist," Iggy went on, "unless we come together as a family and decide to do something about it."

"Uncle Iggy, what is your deal?" said Yogi. "You're like that dude with the peg leg and the whale."

"She means Captain Ahab," said his cousin, Albertina, who was a quiet sort, and the most bookish one in the family.

There was a titter amongst his relatives. Iggy ignored that. He was used to them not understanding him.

"I am not like Captain Ahab," said Iggy, and he paused for a moment to bite down on the joke about harpoons that he wanted so desperately to make to his niece. For someone who was comfortable enough with her body to let her stomach hang all over the place, Yogi was awfully sensitive about it, too. "I just feel that I need to make every effort here, because once we go down this path, we can't undo it. Angela's has been in our family for four generations. Once it's done, it's done. It can't be brought back."

"We *know*!" said his mother, who had mysteriously become unmuted. He slapped the remote against his palm in case the batteries were loose. "That's the whole point! Iggy, it's time to sell!"

"I am reminded of Ecclesiastes," said his Uncle Tom, a

short, balding man with gold-rimmed glasses. "To every-thing there is a season...a time to break down, and a time to build up." Tom had wanted to become a priest, Iggy remem-bered; he had dropped out of the seminary at some point during the '60s and become a librarian instead, but he'd never lost that religious air some people seemed born with.

Iggy had not expected to have the Bible quoted at him. He felt outflanked. Once the opposition started flinging religious quotes at you, you were in trouble. It was time to break out the dirty tricks.

He rushed to the back of the room, removed the oval-shaped portrait of Aniela in her wedding dress from the wall, and carried it back at chest level.

"I just want you all to look at this picture one last time," he said.

"Why one last time? We're not getting rid of the *picture*, Iggy," said Veronica. "We're just getting rid of the *restaurant*!"

"This is Aniela, and she is the reason we're all sitting here today," Iggy said.

"We *know*!" roared several people all at once.

Iggy swallowed. The picture wasn't going to have the effect he'd hoped. He set it on the table in front of the giant television, obscuring half of his father's face.

"The ring, then," Iggy said.

Someone groaned. He suspected it was Yogi. He took off his wedding ring and held it up.

"Does everyone remember the story of the ring?" he asked.

"Do we remember? We have it tattooed on our souls," said Harry.

"Maybe the children don't," said Iggy. "Kids, listen up."

Iggy opened his mouth to launch once more into the story of his wedding ring, which was one that had been retold year after year since 1980, and which people had at first listened to with interest, then with a polite nod, then with a glazed expression. It was a good story, but even a good story can be overtold, and now it tended to elicit avoidant behaviors in those who had heard it ten or eleven times. Several people stood up now, as if they had suddenly remembered doctor's appointments.

"Hey," said Iggy. "Where is everyone going? We still need to vote."

"All in favor of selling, say aye," said Iggy's father from the television.

"Aye," came dozens of voices at once.

"All opposed?"

"Nay," said Iggy.

"The ayes have it," said Big Stosh.

There was more applause, then some hand-shaking. There was nothing for Iggy to do but stand and watch as people began to leave.

Harry came up and placed a hand on his shoulder.

"Iggy," he said kindly, "a word of advice from your brother."

"Yeah, Harry?"

"Know when to give up."

Iggy twisted his ring on his finger.

"It's not over till it's over, Harry," he said.

"Iggy. It's over. I understand why you're trying so hard. I really do. And maybe you're worried because you don't know what you're going to do with yourself. You're a smart guy, Iggy. You'll land on your feet. You could get a job managing any restaurant in this town."

"And work for someone else?"

"I work for someone else. It's not that bad. A lot less headaches. You know what they say about running your own business. It's working eighty hours a week for yourself so you don't have to work forty hours a week for some other guy."

"No way," said Iggy.

"Start your own business, then."

"I already have a business."

"A *new* business. One that's all yours. The point is, Iggy, one door closes, another door opens. We got good news today. And it's not fair, you torturing everyone else like this just because you can't see what's coming next. Everyone else is ready to let go. The world is a different place than it was when Angela's was started."

Iggy nodded.

"Iggy," said Harry. "Let it go. For your own sake. It's what everyone else wants. Everyone except you, apparently." Harry patted him on the shoulder. For a moment the pat turned into more of an open-handed strike, the unconscious meaning of which was not lost on Iggy. Then his brother left.

"Okay, meeting over," he said to the now-empty room. "Thanks for coming, everybody."

He went back into the kitchen. He wanted to be alone, but he had no way to lock the door. So he went into the cooler.

Maybe the chilly air in there would shock him out of what he was feeling right now, which was the overwhelming urge to burst into tears.

What was the matter with him, anyway? Why couldn't he just accept that it was time to move on? They stood to make a decent sum from the sale of the property. It would be a huge weight removed from around their necks. No one besides him had any interest in running a restaurant any longer. Nobody in Buffalo wanted Polish food, not the way they served it. And the thing that had consumed him for decades now, that had kept him awake countless nights, would be removed.

There would be a huge vacuum, then. He could sense it looming in front of him, a Nietzschean abyss. He remembered that expression from his few semesters of classes at Canisius College: if you stare into the abyss long enough, it stares back into you, or something. He couldn't remember. He should probably look it up, but he realized, standing there shivering in the cooler, that he didn't actually give a damn about philosophy quotes, and never had. All he ever wanted to do was sell a plate of pierogies to a table full of hungry people and make them forget for a few moments that the world was a cold place.

The cooler was a cold place, too. But his brother's words had chilled him right to the bone. Go to work for someone else? Was he insane? How did one even go about applying for a job that would replace your life's work? It was easy for Harry to talk. He had hardly worked at Angela's, except for summers in college.

Iggy sat down on a plastic five-gallon bucket of olives. He buried his face in his hands and hoped that no one would walk in on him.

At that moment, his cell phone rang.

"Hello," he said into it.

"It's me," said a voice. "It looks like your wife is about to leave."

Iggy tried to ignore the other, deeper chill that ran through his veins every time he talked to this woman. He still couldn't believe that he had stooped this low. She belonged to a segment of society that was venerable and ancient. For as long as there had been people, there had probably been people like this. Her kind was a necessary part of existence. But up until very recently, Iggy had had nothing to do with this class of person. If it wasn't for books and movies, he would scarcely have known they existed. Just talking to her felt wrong.

"Okay," said Iggy.

"You still want me to go ahead with this?"

Iggy remained silent. His brain was spinning.

"Because once you cross that line, there's no going back," the woman said.

"I know," said Iggy. "Believe me, I know."

"You a Bible-reading man, Iggy?"

"That seems like a strange question for someone in your line of work to be asking." What was this, he asked himself—Bible-quoting day?

The woman chuckled.

"I'm thinking of the Book of Genesis," she said. "The part

where Adam and Eve eat the apple. You remember why the apple was forbidden?"

Iggy shrugged into the phone.

"Because God didn't want us knowing stuff?"

"Because it was fruit of the tree of knowledge of good and evil," said the woman. "Because once you know something, you can't un-know it. That's the line humanity crossed, eons ago. Or six thousand years ago, if you're one of those crazy-ass fundamentalists. You're not one of those, are you, Iggy?"

"No," said Iggy.

"Good," said the woman. "I hate those people. You have my money?"

"Yes. I have it."

"Okay. When it's done we'll do the handoff."

"How will I find you?"

"You won't," said the woman. "I'll find you."

7. BLACK ROCK (DECEMBER 1915)

Aniela stood at the stove in the kitchen of her home. It was a December day, the kind when the air outside felt like the stiff bristles of a brush swiping across one's face. She stirred the coals into life. It was early morning, time to make breakfast for herself...and her husband.

The thing that she thought would never come to pass had happened: she had stood at the altar of Our Lady of Assumption Church in Black Rock and taken vows of holy matrimony. She even had the picture to prove it. It hung on the wall in their tiny parlor. She looked at it often, because it felt to her like a dream: there they were, side by side, dressed in the finest clothes they could afford. Her husband had insisted that another picture be taken of her alone, in her wedding dress. She kept that one in the closet, because it felt vain to have it. It was an extravagance. But she would not deny that every once in a while, when no one else was around, she brought it out to look at it just for a moment.

His name was Jan Podbielski. He, too, was Polish, of course—but of Ruthenian descent, on his mother's side. He came from the Austrian part of the country, or should she say the part that had been stolen by the Austrians when Poland was divided up like a blanket between Austria, Prussia, and Russia.

Aniela had thought life under the Prussians was bad enough, but under the Austrians it was apparently far worse. Jan did not like to talk about it much, but she could tell from the occasional comment that they had been brutal to Poles, that life there had been very rough, and that it had scarred him forever.

Yet there was a side to him that seemed untouched by all that, and this was what Aniela loved about him most. At five feet seven inches, Jan was not a physically imposing man, though he towered a full five inches over her. But he was charismatic, ready to laugh at the drop of a hat, and he could fill a room with his personality the moment he entered it. There was no sadness about him. It seemed to slide off him the way snow slid off a warm roof.

He was unusual for another reason, too: he scarcely touched the vodka that seemed to be the curse of so many other Polish families, especially among the men who labored in the factories six and seven days a week.

Maybe that was because Jan was not a factory worker. He worked with his brains, not his hands, and he felt that he had to stay sharp all the time. Nobody trusted a man who drank too much. He was a business-minded man, always negotiating this, planning that, checking into financing here, forging business connections there. While he was not wealthy—yet—he had an excellent head on his shoulders, and everyone agreed he was going to be a great success one day. Already he owned a small share in a Polish grocery store in Black Rock, and in addition to that, he was constantly turning one small deal after another, pocketing a dollar in profit on Monday, two dollars on Tuesday, as he gradually built up a stake to make his first real foray into business. He had already saved nearly one thousand dollars of his own, he confided to Aniela. For a man who had arrived in America with only ten dollars in his pocket, that was pretty good. But it was only a start. It was the first trickle in what he promised her would eventually become a flood of wealth. And she had no doubt that it was true.

They had met at church, which was a sign that their union was blessed from the beginning. What Jan saw in her, Aniela had no idea. She was aware of the stares of men on the street, but she never thought of herself as beautiful. That would have been vain. Not like Jadwiga, who had constantly primped herself as if expecting a dozen beaus on the front porch.

But Jan had been drawn to her from the moment they first saw each other in the vestibule one Sunday morning after Mass. This was the place where everyone gathered after the service to talk. Dozens of people, all speaking Polish—it was easy to forget that they were in America. For Aniela, this was the best time of the week. She still felt pure, cleansed by the words and magical rituals of the priest chanting in Latin. The sounds of the various dialects of her language being spoken felt as comfortable as her mother's hands braiding her hair. She had the chance to catch up with friends and acquaintances who lived nearby, all of whom were working as hard as she and her sisters. Their busy schedules left little time for socializing…and certainly not much for courting, either.

He hadn't been so bold as to speak to her directly. If he had, she would have written him off at once. No self-respecting woman would go with any man who struck up a conversation with her. But she could sense him looking, hat in hand, as he stood talking to a stranger. When she accidentally-on-purpose glanced his way, he was ready, meeting her eye boldly and smiling. It was just forward enough to be almost scandalous. But that was as far as he took it.

They played this game for several Sundays in a row. At first she had ignored him, hoping he would just go away. But he hadn't. Then she found herself wondering midweek whether he would be there again the next Sunday, and if so, if he would look at her again. He always had. The last time, she was sure he was going to speak to her. He even walked bravely across the vestibule, heading right for her. She steeled herself for his introduction, even as her heart sank, knowing she would have to turn him down.

Instead, he'd done something rather savvy: he introduced himself to Zofia. She had to admit that was clever of him. It showed he had respect for traditional values. Zofia had instantly sized him up as one of the rare good ones worth hanging onto.

"You will never do better," said Zofia to her daughter, later that afternoon, when they were back home. "And you are far too old to be playing hard to get. At your age, you should have been married years ago. You should have children by now. People are wondering what's wrong with you."

"Nothing is wrong with me. I just don't want to get married," said Aniela.

"Why not?"

She shrugged. "I just don't," she said.

She knew she could never bring herself to tell her mother the truth. The very idea of a man putting his hands on her filled her with revulsion and rage.

But she also should have known that her mother could see through her like a pane of glass. Zofia was not a gentle woman. Life had been too hard for that. But she was not cruel, either. If anything, her greatest fault was her practicality.

"We have to remember that we have left a great deal behind us," she told her daughter. "Both good and bad."

"Mostly bad," said Aniela bitterly.

"Yes. So shouldn't we be all the more grateful that it's behind us now? It's better to forget whatever happened and move on."

"I would like nothing better," said Aniela. "But as hard as I try, I can't forget. The harder I want to forget, the more I remember."

"I know that feeling," said Zofia. "And I know you are not just talking about Prussians, either."

Aniela could not bring herself to look at her mother. The shame she felt was simply too great.

Zofia was not given to displays of tenderness, but she reached out and put her hand on top of her daughter's.

"Nothing that happened to you was your fault," said Zofia. "It was theirs. All theirs."

Aniela couldn't hold it back any longer. She did something

she hadn't done since she was a tiny girl. She fell to her knees before her mother, rested her head in her lap, and burst into tears.

"Why do these things happen?" she sobbed.

"Because men are men," said Zofia, stroking her hair. "And women are women. Beyond that there is no reason. Not all men are like that. There are good ones."

"I don't know any."

"Jan is one," said Zofia.

"But how can I know for sure?"

"Trust your mother."

"I don't want to trust anybody. I just want to be alone!"

"You have to remember why we came here. Did we come just for ourselves? No. What would be the point of that? You must have children, Aniela."

"But why? Why *must* I?"

"Don't think of it as a chore. Think of it as a gift to the world that passes through you. You are just the vessel. And think of the life you are giving them here in Ameryka as a gift, too."

"I can't imagine it," she said.

"You don't have to imagine it. Just let nature take its course," said Zofia. "I want to see you girls married before I die."

Aniela had interpreted this as the kind of fatalistic hyperbole to which her mother was given sometimes. Zofia was still only in her fifties. But in fact she had died shortly afterwards. She'd told no one what she had probably known for some time: cancer was destroying her body. She hadn't wanted to be a burden on her daughters or to eat up their savings with medical treatments, so she had suffered in silence until she couldn't hide it anymore. Then the girls had called the doctor to come. By then it was too late. He left them with a bottle of laudanum and instructions on how to dull the pain. It was just a matter of time.

She was gone a few weeks later. The girls wept to see how her body had been ravaged as they lay it out on the kitchen table to be washed; the voluminous black dress she had taken to wearing, which often caused her to be mistaken for a widow, had hidden her pain from the world. Through that body had passed the bodies of three girls and three boys. Women were truly the vessels that held the world, Aniela thought, as she helped prepare her mother's body for burial.

It was then, sponging the ruined flesh from which she had sprung, caressing the proud and careworn face for the last time, that she realized her mother was right about Jan. She would let nature take its course with this man. To do otherwise would be an affront to the generations that had come before her.

Now the three girls, Jadwiga, Aniela, and Catharina, were on their own. But they had long since ceased to be girls; in fact, they had ceased to be children even before they got on the ship to Ameryka. Catharina, the youngest, was twenty-two and already married. Aniela was about to turn twenty-four. Jadwiga was twenty-six, and married as well. She had quickly met a Polish man who spoke English as good as an American, and did, indeed, drive an automobile, in which he frequently took her riding. Now she had a baby, Casimir, the first of their family to be born in this country...the first full-fledged American citizen their family had ever produced.

But not the last. As she prepared her husband's breakfast, Aniela touched the bulge under her apron. She had gotten pregnant almost immediately after their wedding. The baby would arrive sometime in early spring, at the same time as the lambs and piglets on the farms back in their village.

Things had gotten better than she'd dared hope, faster than she could believe possible. The very floorboards on which she stood belonged to them. She and Jan were no longer boarders or lodgers. They owned this house. Try as she might, she didn't think she would ever get used to that idea.

Their new home was on Ledger Street, slightly closer to the Hertel Avenue streetcar stop. The idea that it was all theirs was astonishing. Jan had gone over the terms of the purchase repeatedly with her, just to be sure she understood. It wasn't just that the idea of this strange thing called a *mortgage* was complicated. It was too good to be true.

The banker, a pleasant man with absolutely immense mustaches, had been patient with her. He seemed to understand her concerns, and she had the impression that he had this same conversation several times a week with nervous Polish immigrants. For good measure, and for moral support, Aniela had brought her sisters and her mother with her. She understood that business was the province of men and that she had no right to open her mouth during the meeting. But Jan had told her she could ask questions. He did not lord his maleness over her; he seemed to genuinely want her to understand. It was yet another thing about him that seemed almost strange, considering how different it was from the other men she'd known in her life.

"When you put your money down, you will own a percentage of the house," the banker said in his Warsaw dialect, which they understood with some trouble. "Say, ten percent. The bank will pay the owner the balance, which means the bank owns the other ninety percent. The bank allows you to take possession of the house, which means you can live there. You then pay the bank back everything they spent, plus interest. When the payments are all made, the house is yours. If for some reason you were to stop making payments, the bank will take possession of the house and you will lose it."

The notion that they might lose the house terrified her. If that happened, it would mean they were bankrupt, and that in turn meant they could be deported back to Poland.

But Jan told her not to worry about that.

"I will never let such a thing happen," Jan told her. "And the rest of the community would never let that happen to us. We help each other out."

Aniela was adamant that she would rather go back to Poland than accept charity; and she would rather die than go back to Poland. This resulted in a simple equation: losing the house would mean death. Regardless of the weather, regardless of her health, regardless of whether she had eaten anything that morning or how she was feeling, she would go to work.

But now, Jan would not allow her to work, because of her condition. He made a good living for both of them, and there was plenty to do around the house. It felt strange not going to work every day. And it had taken her a long time to entrust her future to the hands of a man when she had sworn up and down to herself that she would never make that mistake again.

She felt Jan's arms encircle her from behind. He had snuck up on her again. He was very good at that. He had spent his childhood hunting in the mountains, and he was quieter than a cat sneaking up on a mouse.

"How many more days until the baby?" he asked her. This was the same thing he asked her every morning. It was partly a joke, but she could tell he also really believed that she knew the answer.

"The baby will come when the baby comes," Aniela said. "How many days until you are a wealthy businessman?"

"I already am wealthy, if you count my blessings," said Jan. He sat at the table. "But it will be less than a year before I open the new store on Delaware Avenue with Piotr. And after that, you can buy as many dresses as you want."

"Don't be stupid," said Aniela. "I already have two. How many dresses does one woman need?" She spooned some scrambled eggs onto a slice of buttered toast and put it on a plate along with a slab of smoked bacon. Jan liked to eat well in the mornings, because he scarcely touched food for the rest of the day. He was too busy to eat, he said; and besides that, he had a sensitive stomach. He got headaches, too, which sometimes kept him in bed for days. But he hadn't had one of those in a while.

"How should I know? Don't ask me to explain women," he said. "I just know you like nice things."

Aniela thought of the szlachcianka back in the village. How many dresses had she owned? A dozen, probably. What foolishness. Maybe silly girls like Jadwiga aspired to own lots of clothing. For her, what allowed her to sleep well at night was knowing that no Prussians were going to harass them in the streets, no bankers were going to take away their house, no American police were going to carry her off and put her back on the boat to Poland, and her husband was strong enough to defend them against anything. Of course, that didn't stop her from worrying about these things anyway. But it was a comforting kind of worry.

Jan understood America much better than she did. He spoke good English, and he had the respect of many business-men throughout the city. It was his second time to America, in fact. The first time, when he was seventeen, he came for just a year. He had returned to Austrian Poland because his father had died, and he had to make sure that things were properly settled for his mother and siblings. But he had come back again at the age of nineteen, and this time he stayed. He changed his name to John, so that Americans wouldn't find him too strange. He worked very hard at the grocery store of which he was part owner, but he also worked hard in other ways, buying consignments of goods on his own and resell-ing them, seeking the best possible terms for deals, accept-ing small commissions for arranging other contracts, and all manner of other things that she knew nothing about.

Aniela did not care to involve herself with the doings of men. She kept this to herself out of respect for her husband's feelings, but business seemed terribly boring and silly to her, all the more so because men behaved as if what they did all day was so important. Mostly, it seemed to her, they just tried to convince each other, and themselves, of how important they were. Jan could make all the money he wanted, but being a man, he could not make and keep a home. That was her work, her duty; and now that she had followed her mother's advice and "let nature take its course," she realized that it was really all she wanted.

So she was to be the wife of a grocery store owner. This never could have happened in Poland. One did not simply decide to stop being a peasant and join the merchant class. There was much more to it than opening a business. There was the small matter of there being a thousand years of poverty, ignorance, and prejudice to overcome, not to mention that no one could get ahead without paying plenty of bribes to the authorities.

Sometimes, when she thought of the vast distance she had traveled across the face of the earth, and also of how far she had come from the scared, dirty little farm girl she was just a few short years ago, her knees felt weak and she had to sit down. It was almost too much to think about. Better just to forget about that, she told herself for the thousandth time. There was nothing to be gained from looking into the past. It was always better to keep both feet rooted firmly in the present and to have one eye cast toward the future...especially when the future seemed so particularly bright.

She served Jan his plate of breakfast and then leaned back against the counter, hands folded under her belly, watching him eat. How different he was from her father or brothers!

He ate neatly, without grotesque amounts of noise, and with a napkin tucked into his shirt so that nothing dripped on him. When he wanted something, he asked for it politely, rather than demanding it. After he was finished, he buttoned on his stiff collar and put on his hat, checking himself in the mirror. And when he left for the day, Aniela felt not relief, but a pang of regret. Before he was even halfway down Ledger Street, she began looking forward to the moment when he would be home again.

Aniela removed some of the sourdough from the crock it sat in and began mixing up a new batch of dough. She had promised her sisters she would bake them some *chleb zwykly na zakwasie* for them to sell.

Since Zofia had died, they'd continued her sideline business of making various baked goods. They took turns doing the baking every third week. The other two were in charge of selling. They split the money three ways. It was never much, just a bit of pocket change. But it was always good to have a little money coming in from a new direction.

She smiled to remember the first time Jan had noticed the crock of sourdough on the sideboard in the kitchen. He had stared as she fed it, stirring in a bit of molasses and some water, and burst into laughter when she spoke to it as if it were a person. But he understood what it meant to her. He even thought it was a great idea for her to sell her baked goods.

Jan had promised her that once he got his own grocery business underway, they would sell her bread there. It would be very popular. They could claim without lying that it came direct from Poland. Buffalo Poles would line up around the block for a taste of home, he said.

Yet he didn't want her working now. Now, she had a husband to look after her. It would be an insult to him if she were to try to earn her own living. People would say he was not capable of supporting his family. She baked now almost as a hobby. She loved the feel of the dough in her hands, and she loved how it reminded her of her mother and grandmother mixing the dough together in their tiny kitchen back home in Poland, then taking the dough to the baker for him to bake in the communal oven.

While her hands worked the dough, she gradually taught herself to think not of all the things they had lost, but of all the things that were to come.

8. KENMORE (SEPTEMBER 2015)

Silvestra made the drive to Grand Island that afternoon, while everyone else was in the family meeting. She had no interest in such things. For one, she actively detested most of Iggy's family. It wasn't that they had ever done anything to offend her. It was that she was desperately bored with them, and the restaurant, and everything.

For another, the restaurant was doomed. The ship was going down. Anyone who didn't hop into a lifeboat now deserved to drown. Sure, it had sustained them all these years, but nothing was forever.

So now what?

Well, something would occur to her, she was certain. She hadn't thought too hard about what would come next. There seemed no need. In a way, these things took care of themselves, didn't they?

She had been making this drive every Thursday for the past five months. Nearly six, she thought. They were coming up on an anniversary of sorts. It was nowhere near as long as she had been with Iggy, but that was the whole point, wasn't it? She was starting over. It felt indescribably good to be sloughing off the past, like a snake shedding its old skin. So her mother wouldn't have approved. So she was committing a sin. Who cared? Sometimes you had to make your own rules. If there was one thing she'd learned, it was that the rules were all made by men. Even religion was invented by men as a way to keep people in line. Well, she was done living like that. From now on, Silvestra did as Silvestra pleased.

She paid cash for the motel room, like always. At first, during her early visits, she had gone to the trouble of wearing a kerchief on her head and a pair of dark glasses, but she felt like that just called more attention to her. And no one seemed to care what she was doing. The clerk, an overweight woman in her early thirties, appeared so bored by the whole transaction that Silvestra almost felt sorry for her.

She felt sorry for just about everyone these days. Maybe someday this lady would be lucky enough to have this kind of excitement in her life, she thought. If she lost a little weight, that is.

She climbed the shuddering cement stairs to the second-floor room and primped herself in the bathroom. She put on the silk robe he seemed to like so much, judging from the way he ran his hands over her whenever she was wearing it. Then she lay on the bed and clicked on her smartphone to distract herself.

He knocked a few minutes later.

"It's open," she called, feigning disinterest.

He walked in without bothering to greet her. It was funny to her that he still wore a hat, such as men in previous generations had worn. In so many ways, he was a very progressive man, always thinking about how to shape the future. He was certainly going to shape *her* future. But he dressed like it was 1950. She had never been able to figure out if this was style or stubbornness.

At least he took his hat off when he was indoors. He tossed it now on the table and sat down on the edge of the bed to take off his shoes.

"Hard day?" she said.

"I've had better," said Schroder.

"Come to Silvie," said Silvestra. "I'll make you feel better."

Schroder grunted. "You always do," he said.

"That's right. Come on."

Schroder crawled onto the bed on all fours. Then he crawled on top of her. He barely gave her time to get ready for him, so eager was he suddenly to show her what a man he was. When she was about to tell him to slow down, he covered her mouth with his hand, the way she had asked him to do once on a whim and which he had done every time since then. She didn't like it every time, but it seemed to get him so excited she was afraid to tell him to stop.

She wondered what went through his mind when he did that to her. She thought she had a pretty good idea. Sometimes it excited her that he was such an animal. Other times it sent a flutter of panic through her. But even that was exciting, as long as he didn't cross the line he kept walking up to and deliberately sticking his toe over.

"My goodness," she said, when it was all over and he let her speak again. "Where did that come from?"

"I'm feeling good," said Schroder. "Like I'm twenty years younger." He rolled off her. He hadn't even bothered to remove his pants all the way, and he arched his back now as he pulled them back up and refastened his belt buckle.

"A quickie?" she sniffed.

He looked at her sideways. "You said you liked those," he reminded her.

"Sometimes I might like to spend a little time with you."

"Jesus, Sil," said Schroder. "I got enough people after me all day long."

She fell silent. Perhaps he felt bad then, because he reached over and took her hand, holding it up and toying with it, as though it belonged to a mannequin or something. She willed it to remain inanimate. After a moment he dropped it.

"What's bugging you?" he asked.

She shrugged. "A lot of things are just changing, that's all," she said.

"What do you mean?"

She didn't have the energy or the desire for an argument, and that was what would surely result if there was a confrontation now. So she gave in, again, and made it about something else. The last thing on earth she actually wanted to talk about, as it happened. But she couldn't bear the idea of a fight. Not when she had been feeling so good earlier.

"At home. At the restaurant."

"Oh yeah. The restaurant." Schroder appeared to become unusually thoughtful for a moment. "Is he still gonna sell the place?"

"He doesn't want to. But he has no choice. Everyone else has voted."

"Hmm." Schroder stared reflectively at the ceiling. "Anybody lined up to buy it?"

"He's been awfully close-lipped about that," said Silvestra. "He doesn't want anyone to know."

"Well, everyone in the family knows, don't they? Someone must be talking about it."

"I don't know." She prodded him. "You should buy it," she said.

"And do what with it? What do I need with a restaurant?"

"You could do anything with it," Silvestra said.

"And then you would get your money," Schroder said. "Right? And then everyone would get their money."

"Gee," said Silvestra. She made sure he could hear the hurt in her voice. What did he think of her, anyway?

Schroder said nothing more. After a while she heard heavy breathing. He had fallen asleep.

Silvestra rolled over on her side. She would lie here a moment longer, she decided, then get up and freshen herself. Then, if he wasn't awake yet, she would simply leave. What would she do with the rest of her evening? There was a queue of shows waiting for her in her Netflix account, and there was three-quarters of a bottle of white wine chilling in the fridge at home. She felt herself growing cozy and warm at the thought of these indulgences. Suddenly there, and not here, was where she longed to be.

She slid out of bed as quietly as possible. Let him wake up in an empty motel room. She could not imagine anything more deflating than that. He needed a pin to prick his ego, she thought. She was not going to call him, text him, e-mail him, anything. Maybe after a week without her he would change his tune. Be a little more respectful of her. She was going to have to play him that way if things were going to work out the way she wanted them to.

Because it was Schroder she intended to hitch her wagon to, when all this restaurant nonsense was over. He was not stuck in the past, like Iggy. He was a visionary. He put up blocks of housing all over town, sold them, made a fortune. He was already a millionaire. She would leave Iggy, Schroder would leave his wife, and they would be together. It was already proven that they made each other happy.

She got dressed and stepped outside the motel room, into the crosshairs that were trained on her from the parking lot.

9. BLACK ROCK (DECEMBER 1920)

Aniela had never understood why people asked whether there was a God or not. Of course there was a God. If not, who else had made the vast world, and all the astonishing and beautiful things in it? Who had made the wide ocean she'd had to travel across to come to this confusing and amazing country? Who had made it possible for her to have the miracle of her first baby, a little girl, now four years old and a bouncing mass of golden curls? Who had made it possible for the miracle of life to be growing within her a second time? A boy this time, she was sure.

And who else but God would have taken her husband from her on the day after Christmas, in a burst of horribly cruel irony, when everything had been going so perfectly?

Whose master plan was it that Aniela would come out into the kitchen late on the evening of the twenty-sixth to find out why Jan hadn't come to bed yet, and would see him lying on the floor, unmoving, his face terrifying in its lack of expression, one arm stretched in the direction of the bedroom, as if he had been trying to crawl toward her?

She did not remember screaming. But she must have, for somehow the upstairs tenants knew to come pounding down the stairs and force their way into the house. Then the next-door neighbors on either side had arrived, carrying kerosene lamps and candles in wind protectors. More people had come, hearing the commotion. Suddenly, the house was full of people.

It was St. Stephen's Day, the day when they used to bless the grain for the coming season of growth. Though they had no grain to bless and no fields to plant it in, it was still a day of celebration for many Poles who remembered life on the farm. It was a party that went on all day. Several of them were still dressed in their finer clothes, groggy from wine or vodka.

It was too late to save Jan; no amount of calling his name, of slapping him on his cheeks, of pressing on his chest, brought him back. He did not respond to smelling salts, a dash of icy water in his face, or a shot of vodka poured down his throat.

He was gone. God had called him home.

The tragedy sharpened everyone. These Poles were not the kind of people to stand around dumbly, trying to figure out what to do next. At such moments their instincts and traditions kicked in. They were accustomed to tragic incidents, to sudden loss, to incomprehensibly cruel fate. They knew the most important rule of all in times like this: keep moving.

The second most important rule was: the ones who had not suffered must help the ones who had, for someday, those roles would be reversed.

What happened after that, Aniela really did not remember. The women had forced her to go back to her bed, so as not to further disturb the baby that grew within her. They were afraid the shock of finding Jan would cause her to abort. Several women sat with her as she lay on her side, staring numbly at the wall, fighting tears. What good would crying do? And yet what else was there to do?

The neighbors had taken little Agnieszka with them. Aniela could hear her daughter wailing as they left, and she had wanted to go to her but felt as if she was trapped in mud up to her neck. She could not move or breathe. Was Jan really dead? Was the whole thing not just a bad dream? How could a man so young and healthy be felled so suddenly, with no warning, with not even a sound to warn her?

It was those damned Prussians, she thought wildly. They'd found out where they were and cut him down with poison. Or no, it was the Austrians. Or the Russians. Who had they thought they were, these lowly Poles, living as if they were nobles? Daring to own a home, to save money, to rise up out of the mud? Their old oppressors had wanted to teach them a lesson. That was the only explanation.

But this made no more sense than any of the other thoughts flitting through her head like rabid bats.

It was God, then. God had grown angry with them for rising too high above their station. He had punished her for her sinful thoughts—dreaming of fine things, daring to believe she was anything more than a peasant girl.

As the sun rose, a doctor came for Jan, though it was plain there was nothing he could do. It was most likely an aneurysm, he'd said. Aniela did not know what that was. Someone explained it to her: a blood clot. Jan would never have known it was coming. He would have felt nothing.

The doctor gave her something to help her sleep. It tasted like fire and brimstone, but it knocked her out.

And now, here it was, the next day, and the coffin was arranged on sawhorses in the front room. Once upon a time, right here in this room, she had hoped to entertain the wives of the men Jan did business with. Georg Stefanek, Jan's business partner in the grocery, had come here several times with his bride, and she and Aniela had listened and smiled at each other while the men drank coffee and giggled over their future like two excited schoolboys.

Someone had taken down the Christmas tree to make room for the coffin. Aniela was grateful for that. It did not seem fitting to have a symbol of celebration in a room of mourning, although Jan himself would have found the contrast pleasing, and perhaps even amusing. He always had a way of pointing out things like that. *Look, Ani, isn't it funny?* he might have said. *A tree with ornaments, right next to a dead man. Isn't life just like that?*

Inside the coffin was Jan, looking utterly like himself on this cold December day, as if he was merely asleep and playing a cruel joke. The women who prepared his body had done a careful job. His hair was neatly combed, and his face and lips were lightly rouged, to disguise the terrible paleness of death. He wore the same fine suit he'd worn on their wedding day. On his finger glinted his wedding ring, a plain, thick band he'd had inscribed with their initials and the date of their wedding: *A.L. to J.C. June 16, 1915.*

She looked at his hands. They had always seemed massive to her. They dwarfed her own, which were none too small to begin with. His hands were always moving: fixing or building something, writing something down, gesturing, perhaps even touching her own hands or running them through her hair, as he sometimes did for no reason. Now they lay neatly folded across his middle, idle for the first time since she had known him. What would she give to see him open those eyes and step out of his wooden bed? What kind of bargain would she be willing to make for her own immortal soul, for the sake of her little girl and the one who grew within her?

She shuddered. She had felt desperate before, but never like this. Now she understood how people could contemplate making deals with the Devil.

She crossed herself and made a mental note to go to confession as soon as possible. The priest would tell her that grief-stricken thoughts were to be expected, and that she was likely to have all sorts of strange ideas until she grew used to her status as a widow. He would tell her to stop fighting and surrender to the will of God, and other things that deep down she already knew. But he would also do for her what she could not do for herself: he would absolve her of her sins and cleanse her soul again.

At least she had her sisters. They knew better than to try to make her forget her sadness. They understood that she would have to move through it on her own terms. She could hear them now, in the kitchen, talking quietly between themselves and to the children.

The children had grown up around their ankles like a field of American flowers. Jadwiga had two boys, Casimir and Maximilian, and Catherina had a boy and a girl, Joseph and

Helen. With Agnieszka, that made five children born here in America, natural Americans who would never have to worry about being deported; and as soon as this newest baby arrived, there would be six.

A new baby. A hundred times already this thought had swirled around her head—once a pleasant sense of antici-pation, now a nightmare. How would she deal with a baby? Who would support her? It simply wasn't possible for a woman to make it on her own. No job would ever pay her enough to keep them from relying on charity. She couldn't become a burden on her sisters. She could not accept alms from the church.

Her only option was to remarry, as soon as possible.

But the thought made her blood run cold. It had taken her years to prepare herself mentally to marry this man. She had only agreed to do so because of his innate goodness. Because he was not a barn animal and not a wolf, but a decent person. There were no more out there like him, or very few, anyway. She would never remarry.

Maybe she should kill herself, taking the baby with her. She could go to the great thundering Falls and throw her-self over. It would be terrifying, but it would be over quickly. Agnieszka would be raised by her sisters. After a while she wouldn't even remember Aniela. It would be a gift to her daughter—erasing the tragedy of her childhood in one self-less act, so that she could grow up in a household with two parents.

Or maybe she should take Agnieszka with her. Then all their suffering would be ended.

More horribly sinful thoughts. She seemed full of them. Of course she was not going to kill herself. Did she think that she knew the will of God? The Lord despised a murderer and a suicide. She would be buried in unconsecrated ground, she and the baby inside her...if her body was even found, that is. Plenty of jilted lovers and girls in trouble had thrown themselves into the river and were never seen again, their bodies eaten by fishes, their bones green with algae and bouncing lonely among the stones on the riverbed, where no one would ever come to visit them.

She crossed herself once more. She longed to tell Jadwiga and Catherina about the torment she was in. But she worried they would think she was possessed by an evil spirit and have her locked up. Who else but a crazy person would have these thoughts?

Yet another terrifying specter began to swirl before her: deportation. Would the American government not decide that she was a burden, now that she had no man to take care of her?

I must not become a burden, she thought.

More than that—she must succeed. She must find a way to do it somehow. But how?

This was the question she asked herself as they sat in silence in the house during the wake. There was a long line of people waiting outside to come in and pay their respects. Georg and Annika Stefanek walked in somberly and bowed low before Jan's body. Annika embraced her. Georg took her hand for a long moment and held it, and she could see that his eyes were full of tears. There was no talk from him now of a happy future. His own dreams had just been dashed as well.

Person after person bowed and knelt before what was left of Jan. He had been well liked and respected. There was a small bowl near his coffin where several neighbors left envelopes. She could hear the jingle of coins in them. The sound mortified her. What must they think of her—that she was a beggar now? She would give it all back, every cent. Or she would give it to the church, to care for the poor.

The house, she remembered suddenly. The house was still hers. There were still tenants paying rent upstairs. The bank would not take it from her if she kept up the payments. If she could just manage to do that, they would survive.

Soon the undertaker came in his wagon, accompanied by the priest. She watched as the priest scooped up the envelopes in the bowl and tucked them inside his cassock. That answered the question of what to do with the money. Well, she had only been going to donate it anyway. The priest knew the will of God, not she.

Everyone left the house and got into one of the long line of automobiles on the street. It seemed strange to her to ride in style like this to a cemetery. It was wrong. This was a time for simplicity and humility, not putting on grand airs. Back home they would have walked the whole way, the coffin riding on the shoulders of the men. But this was the way it had been arranged. This is how things were done in America.

They were going to St. Stanislaus Cemetery, in the strangely-named Cheektowaga. It was not so far that they couldn't have walked, though it would have been a hard journey. But here in America, you did everything in your horseless carriage. The invention that Zofia had been sure would never amount to anything had already changed the city. Horses were becoming a rarity. You looked twice when you saw one now. How quickly things changed.

Once everyone had left the house, the undertaker and his men loaded the coffin into the hearse. Then Aniela and her sisters got into another car, a long black one, without doubt the finest automobile she had ever seen.

"Look at us, riding in an automobile together," Catherina remarked to her and Jadwiga. "What would Mother say?"

Aniela did not smile, but she appreciated her effort at a joke. It reminded her that life went on.

"Did you remember to get his ring?" Jadwiga asked Aniela suddenly.

Aniela stared out the window as the hearse pulled away. She felt as if she weighed a thousand pounds.

"No," she said. Jan's wedding ring was still on his finger, in the coffin.

"Shall we stop him? It's not too late."

"Let him keep it," she said. "I had no money to pay him anyway."

Jadwiga and Catherina both understood: she was referring to the undertaker. He had to be paid somehow. He had children of his own to feed. He had not even mentioned cost when he was summoned to the house. He had simply gone about his trade, measuring Jan for his coffin, then hurrying home to build it without delay. Maybe now, with Jan's ring in his pocket, he wouldn't hound her for payment.

They drove along behind the hearse, all the way to St. Stanislaus Cemetery. The temperature was well below freezing, and there was half an inch of snow on the ground. Somehow, the cemetery workers had managed to dig a hole. The ground had not completely frozen yet, but it would soon.

They buried Jan in a far corner, all by himself—just the way he had arrived in the New World. Aniela wished this did not give her such a chill. He was never afraid to be on his own, Aniela thought as she cried. He had never complained about the hardships he'd faced under the Austrians, or about his crossing, or about anything at all. He was full of nothing but cheerfulness and optimism.

She listened to the priest chant in Latin as he swung the censer, and they all shivered in the brutal Buffalo cold that had just descended the night before.

Someday I will rest next to you, she vowed silently, and she watched them lower the coffin into the ground. *We will be together again.*

10. SOUTH BUFFALO (SEPTEMBER 2015)

The next morning, Iggy waited in a dingy coffee shop in South Buffalo, where no one knew him. He realized he had chosen a place where he knew he would feel miserable. He needed to be somewhere that looked like how he felt. Miserable coffee served in miserable, chipped, heavy-duty restaurant ware, like you might find in ten thousand diners across the country. He would never have allowed such cups in his restaurant. They had been lifted to ten thousand lips, and they looked it. If you checked carefully, you would find layers of lipstick on each and every one. A cup of coffee should be a pleasant and satisfying experience, not an archaeological expedition. He shook his head. Some people just had no standards.

He'd been surprised that this woman wanted to meet with him in person. In this day and age, when everything could be done zip-zip-zip over the Internet, this was a rarity. She could have just e-mailed him the proof that Iggy had paid her for. But the woman had explained that it was better not to have such things out there.

By "out there" Iggy supposed she meant "on the computer." She had a point. If something was on a computer, it could be e-mailed to somebody, and then it was like grains of sand in the wind of the Internet. You would never get it back. Maybe it could be used as evidence. Who knew? All this stuff was more than he cared to think about. He preferred to leave it for others. Him, all he ever wanted to do was serve a plate of good authentic Polish food to anyone who was hungry. You didn't need a computer to do that.

From the description of herself she'd given him, he could tell right away that she was the woman he was there to meet. She had an air about her, though she was tiny, scarcely five feet, and no spring chicken, either. She was about sixty-five or so, judging by the miles on her face. Iron-gray hair cut short. A Hillary Clinton pantsuit. You looked at her and thought *grandmother*, or maybe *schoolteacher*, or possibly *nun*. You did not think *detective*. But in fact, that was what she was.

She sat in Iggy's booth without hesitating. Iggy wondered how she knew who *he* was, for he had offered her no description of himself. Maybe she had been spying on Iggy, too, just to make sure he was on the level. So he'd been investigated, too. That creeped him out.

"Mr. Podbielski," said the tiny woman.

"Hello there," said Iggy. He felt like he should say something a little more hard-boiled than that, but nothing came naturally to his lips.

"I guess you know who I am," said the woman.

"Yes. I know. Is it done?"

She regarded him with some amusement, a smile wrinkling

the corners of her mouth before she chased it away again. Her face looked like it had been ironed. Iggy had the sense that expressions did not cross it easily, and when she did laugh, it wasn't at things other people would find funny. She was more like a man than a woman in many ways, he thought.

"Yes, it's done."

"You have the proof?"

"You sure you want to see it?"

Iggy felt he was being toyed with. He did not appreciate that. In his experience, whenever he had to deal with recalcitrant employees or angry customers, he found that silence and a fixed gaze did more than anything else to bring them into line quickly. This woman would never be intimidated by him, but at least she would know he wasn't someone he could push around.

"Why wouldn't I want to see it?" he said finally. "I hired you, didn't I?"

The detective shrugged.

"Some people throw a scene," she said. "They put up a fuss. I don't like the drama."

"No drama," said Iggy. "If you're gonna show me, show me."

The woman held up a cell phone and showed him a picture. It was Silvestra, going into a motel room. She was dressed like she thought she was suddenly thirty years younger. Iggy winced. He was actually embarrassed for her. It was pathetic, a woman of that age squeezing into those clothes, like the year was 1985 and she was headed to a Duran Duran concert.

"That's her," said the woman. "Right?"

Iggy nodded.

The detective swiped her finger across the screen and showed another picture. It was Schroeder, going into the same motel room. He was dressed like he was always dressed—like he was either going to or coming from a building site.

"So? You see one going in, then the other going in. How does this prove they were in there together?"

"You want to see the pictures I took through the curtains?" the woman said.

Iggy felt himself grow pale.

"No," he whispered.

Despite the lousy feeling in his stomach, Iggy thought he understood now. For Silvestra, this was some kind of youthful fantasy. She needed to prove to herself she was still desirable. For Schroeder, it was fulfilling a practical need. He had found himself a woman who would satisfy his animal wishes. That this woman happened to be Iggy's wife was maddening, even though it had been a long time since he'd felt that way about Silvestra himself.

"I have about fifty more," said the detective. "You can have all of them. You paid for them. But you get the idea."

Iggy exhaled. Suddenly he had an overwhelming urge to cry.

"I see," he said. "Okay. So I was right."

"It looks that way," she said.

She did not apologize, offer condolences, or say anything remotely philosophical, not that Iggy had been expecting her to. She simply removed a padded envelope from her purse and handed it over.

"That's a disk with all the pictures on it," she said. "After I delete these from my phone, those are the only copies of these photos. You decide what you want to do with them."

Iggy took the envelope and held it on his lap under the table. He felt like the entire restaurant could see through the envelope to its contents. Everyone knew he was being cuckolded by one of the wealthier contractors in the city. A man who was more successful than he was. A man who had just destroyed his marriage.

"Okay," said Iggy.

"They were in there for three hours," said the woman. "Just so you know there's no mistake about why they were there. The photos are all time-stamped. I mention this because sometimes people want to argue with the evidence. They try to convince themselves there's an innocent explanation. Just like you tried a couple of minutes ago."

She shook her head, as if answering her own question.

"There is no innocent explanation," she said. "Things are almost always what they look like."

Iggy couldn't even bring himself to look at her now. He had the devastating impression that this woman had had this same conversation with a thousand spouses. He was just one more monkey in an exhibit, going through all the same pointless things everyone else went through in their lives before they died and shriveled into dust, and all the things they were so worried about didn't matter anymore. There was really nothing special about him at all, was there?

"Anything else before I go?" the woman asked.

"Yeah, there was one thing," Iggy said. "Something I'd like

to know. Is it usually the man who…who cheats? Or is it usually the woman?"

The woman stared at him for a long moment, as if trying to figure out why he would ask such a question. Then she shrugged and looked away.

"It's about the same," she said. "It's basically half and half." Suddenly she nodded, as if she understood the question now: Iggy was wondering if there was someone to blame. "Nobody is innocent here. It takes two to tango, you know."

Iggy nodded too. Somehow, that trite piece of insight made him feel better.

After that, he went home. He felt free. There was no more need for pretending. It was all out in the open now.

Silvestra's car was in the driveway. He knew that he would walk in the front door and hear her watching TV in the family room. He knew that she would not call out a greeting as he came into the house. He knew that if he went into the kitchen he would find a bottle of wine open on the counter, already half gone, even though it was barely afternoon. He knew that if he did not make a point of speaking to her first, she would not say a word to him.

He went upstairs to their bedroom and got his suitcase from the back of his closet. It had been so long since he'd been anywhere that it was covered in dust bunnies. He blew on the suitcase and then wiped it clean with a washcloth.

Then he packed: underwear, pants, shirts, toothbrush, razor, socks, deodorant. He realized he had no idea what he was doing. He was not used to packing. He never went anywhere. He had not left Buffalo in several years. He had never been out of the country, unless you counted the Canadian side of the Falls. The last interesting place he'd been was Florida, about twenty years ago, where he had sat on the beach for a week and fretted about the restaurant. Milwaukee, once, for the funeral of a relative. Traveling was a horrible nuisance. He would never understand why some people liked it so much.

He didn't try to be quiet. He simply performed his tasks as though he had nothing to hide. When his suitcase was packed, he set it down by the front door. Then he went into the kitchen and made himself a sandwich. He was not terribly hungry, but he knew he should eat something. He needed to be at the restaurant in an hour, and he would not eat while he was on duty, whether there were any customers or not. It was unprofessional. If she came out, he would talk to her. But he would not go in there to make a point of telling her.

When he was finished eating, he rinsed his plate and put it in the dishwasher. At the front door he stopped for a moment and looked around the house, or the part of it he could see from there.

They had lived here for twenty-three years.

She had not come out of the television room.

He drove eleven blocks in his car to a house that looked very much like every other house in this part of Buffalo. It was a two-storey house, probably a hundred years old now, with living space for two families, one on each floor. On the left side, a driveway just wide enough for a car separated the place from its neighbor, a house that was essentially identical except for the color of the curtains in the front window. On the right side was an even narrower strip of ground that had not seen the sun in a century. In front was a lawn that was perhaps the size of a large blanket.

He walked up the driveway and knocked on the side door. Len answered. He handed Iggy a key and pointed him upstairs, to the second-floor unit. Iggy climbed the steps and opened the front door. The smells of a thousand long-gone meals drifted out at him. Whoever lived here before him had used a lot of lard and garlic. This would be where he slept from now on, but he would never be able to say that he lived here. He dropped his suitcase inside the front door, locked it again, turned around, and left.

Next he headed for the restaurant. He took Len and Mr. Danny with him in his car, which was an offer he had originally made out of convenience but which he now felt contained a certain amount of symbolism. It was the last day the place would be open, after all.

The three of them did not speak on the journey, which lasted about seven minutes. Mr. Danny sat in the front, his feet barely touching the floor. When they got there, Len opened the door for his father and led him to the kitchen door by the hand, as if he were a small child.

Iggy would have liked there to be some kind of acknowledgement from his family that this was the last day. But none of them had even showed up. Why would they? They were busy, and they didn't care. Their lives had nothing to do with this restaurant anymore, even though they existed because it existed, even though it had fed all of them for decades.

Jesús stood in the parking lot, smoking and talking on his cell phone. When he saw Iggy pull up, he put it back in his pocket.

"Not on your cell phone? You feeling okay?" Iggy asked him. He had meant it to be a joke, but Jesús did not take it that way.

"No, I not," said Jesús. Iggy saw he actually had tears in his eyes.

"Aw," he said. "Don't cry, Jesús. It'll be okay."

"You been a good boss to me," said Jesús. "I gonna miss you." He embraced Iggy, holding him close for an embarrassing moment.

"Jesus, Jesús," said Iggy. "You been into the tequila already?"

"I found another job," said Jesús. "I just wanted you to know."

"What kind of job?"

"Gonna be a sous-chef," said Jesús proudly, wiping his eyes with the back of his hand. "They're gonna train me and everything. Someday I'm gonna own a place just like this."

"You wanna own a restaurant?"

Jesús nodded.

"What are you, crazy? Restaurants are nothing but heartache. It's just a big restaurant-shaped hole in the ground where you throw money. That's all."

"Naw," said Jesús. "Look at you. You got everything, Iggy." Jesús had always had trouble with the double Gs in Iggy's name. He pronounced it *Eee-hee*. "So the place gonna close? You're gonna open another one. I can feel it right here." He pounded himself on the chest. "People like you, Mr. Eee-hee, you always win. I know. I watch you. I learn. You a big help for me. I'm gonna be like you, someday."

Iggy stared at Jesús for longer than he meant to. Was it possible that another human being on this planet actually envied his situation? Such a thought had never occurred to him. He spent most of his time absorbed in misery and self-pity, always wondering how he was going to pull something off, how he was going to get ahead. Jesús had been born in a ghetto in Mexico. Iggy realized that he did not know a thing about what that must have been like. But if he looked at Iggy and saw something to aspire to, it must have been pretty bad.

"Wait. Here," said Iggy. He reached into his pocket and pulled out an envelope he had prepared already. "This is your pay, plus a little extra. You don't need to stick around today, Jesús. Go home to your family. No one will come in anyway."

Jesús looked at him, wide-eyed.

"For reals?"

"Yes. And thank you. For all your hard work, and for saying what you just said. It means a lot." He sighed. "If this place was mine to give, I would give it to you. You've earned it."

"Aw," said Jesús. "Maybe someday I invite you to my restaurant. You be my first guest. I put you in the best table, up front." He put the envelope in his pocket and stuck out his hand.

Iggy shook it. "It's a deal," he said.

Jesús smiled, his gold grillwork gleaming.

11. BLACK ROCK (MARCH 1923)

If anyone were to ask Aniela how she had spent the past three years, she would not be able to tell them. The moments had blended into one another, in much the same way as the faces she saw from the speeding streetcar blurred into one monstrous, leering visage sometimes, a face that seemed to mock her loneliness, her exhaustion, her endless store of fears. Time was just a long stretch of colorless infinity. One moment she'd been the happily pregnant bride of an up-and-coming businessman; the next, she was a widow with two young children and the chapped hands and aching back of a laundress and housecleaner.

It wasn't that she thought she was too good for that kind of work. She did not have delusions about herself. There was just too much of it. If it hadn't been for her sisters, she would have sunk into the earth under the weight of her own exhaustion. This was all she did: change baby bottoms, do other people's laundry, cook, and sleep. Sometimes Jadwiga or Catharina took her children for a few hours so she could get something done around her own household, or just steal a few more moments' rest. But she didn't like to rely on them to carry her burden.

Nothing about life made any sense.

Why was life organized so cruelly, she wondered, with all the strength of youth at one end of it, and the wisdom of old age at the other? It was as if the Creator endowed them with the spark of life, then left them to their own devices, and they spent the rest of their time on earth beseeching Him to step in and save them from their own stupidity.

And why was it that the poor of the world were fated to take care of everyone else except the ones they loved, while the wealthy had to care for no one but themselves, even though they had all the resources of the world at their disposal? This, too, was backwards.

So much about the world seemed broken. And then there were the calamities that happened, one after another. Just a handful of years earlier, a terrible plague had roared across the world. They called it the Spanish Influenza. Hundreds of thousands of people had died in America alone. By some miracle, her own family had been spared. But she knew plenty of people who had lost loved ones. Children and the elderly were the most common victims, but even healthy young men and women had been claimed as well. They died within two or three days of falling ill. It reminded her of stories of horrible plagues sweeping Poland in the time of her ancestors.

The influenza had come at the tail end of yet another war in Europe. This one had lasted four long years. It had been so awful that they simply called it The Great War. Men suffered horribly and died, millions of them. Millions more women and children died as well. She understood enough English now to follow what she read in newspaper headlines. She did not have the time or patience to read the articles themselves, but it didn't matter. War was all anyone had talked about. It seemed like they were living in the worst time in history.

At least now the Hun had been whipped like the dog he was. For the first time since the eighteenth century, Poland could be said to be a nation once again. When they made maps now, they would have Poland on them. Their homeland had been restored.

Some Buffalo Poles had talked about going back home after 1918. But it had never once occurred to Aniela to do so. She'd fled more than the Prussians, after all. The muddy lanes of the village had never held one-tenth the promises as the paved avenues of Buffalo, the City of Light, still among the greatest cities of the world.

She and her sisters received letters from relatives back home. This was how she knew that everything there was still the same: that electricity still had not come to the village; that pigs still wallowed in their own filth, the way they had since time immemorial; that men still expected women to wait on them hand and foot; that though the Prussians were gone now, life had not become much easier.

Go home? That would be madness. She was an American now. So were her sisters and all their children.

There would still be that terrible journey to deal with, the journey she had sworn she would never make again. And her father—if he was still alive—and her brothers would still be there, up to their old barn animal tricks.

Maybe they had all drunk themselves to death by now. That would be a blessing.

There was one bright spot. Her baby brother, Martyn, the only good one of the lot, had finally come to America.

Martyn had just arrived the day before. The sisters had not been able to contain their excitement at seeing him again. They shrieked with joy when he arrived at Aniela's house. It was the first time Aniela had felt real happiness since Jan died. Seeing him made her remember that there was still some joy to be found in being alive. She pressed his face to hers until his cheeks were as wet as her own, and he protested, spluttering, that he couldn't breathe.

The last time she'd seen Martyn, he'd been standing in the doorway of their ramshackle home in Poland, sobbing as his mother and sisters pulled away on the wagon that would take them to the train station. He was fifteen years old then, small for his age, his brow perpetually creased with concern, his manners soft and girlish.

Now he was thirty. He should have become a man by now. But he looked as if he had failed the tests of which manhood consisted. His clothes were threadbare, so he lacked money. His face was drawn and worried, so he lacked confidence. She could tell that the crossing had not been kind to him. But life had been unkind even before that. He looked around furtively, as if constantly expecting a blow from behind. Aniela had privately hoped that his girlish ways would have disappeared as he became older. Other men being the beasts they were, it would have made things so much easier for him. She could see now that this hadn't happened.

Well, she didn't care. That was one of the rules made by the world of men, and the rules of men did not apply in this house any longer. She squeezed him until she felt his ribs creak.

Martyn laughed with joy as he was smothered by his sisters. He wept like a child over the loss of their mother. He hugged his nieces and nephews for the first time and marveled at the fact that they were Americans by birth. He ate food as quickly as it was shoveled into him. He drank the sweet homemade wine they poured for him, glass after glass, to wash away old sadness and bring new happiness. He tried to answer all their questions about what was different now that Poland was free, though still plagued by conflict with its neighbors. Then, finally, he slept the deep slumber of the traveler who has fled across half the world, and who has felt every emotion it is possible for a human to feel within the space of a few hours.

The next day was a Sunday. The whole family—the three sisters, two husbands, their children, and Martyn—went to Mass together at Our Lady of the Assumption. Afterward, they introduced Martyn to the priest, Father Olsafski. He received a special blessing that the sisters fervently hoped would allow him to take root here in the New World without too much suffering. Aniela could tell that he had been instantly appraised by the mothers of all the single girls in the congregation, and almost as quickly rejected. Clothes patched and ragged—one step above pauperism. Shoulders and back stooped—not the attitude of a man who was poised to succeed in life. Not particularly good-looking, either, though if he only stood up straight and looked people in the eye he would be presentable enough. And there was something lacking about him in general, the thing that made women notice men out of the corner of their eye. Whatever that was, he didn't have it.

"There are lots of Polish business owners in Buffalo," Aniela told Martyn as they walked home. "One of them will give you a job. All you have to do is ask."

"I hope so," he said, without much conviction. "Tomorrow, first thing, I will start looking."

"What kind of work have you done?"

He shrugged. "Just chores around the farm," he said.

"How are…things…there?" Aniela asked. She had put off the question this long, but she could not leave it any longer. She could feel Martyn grow tense beside her.

"The same," he muttered. "They are no different."

"Did they help you with the cost of coming over?"

He snorted. "What do you think?"

"Nothing?"

"Anielka. I didn't even tell them I was leaving." He took off his hat, even though they were still outside, and began to twist it in his hands. "Our father is dead," he said finally. "I'm sorry I didn't mention it sooner. I just couldn't bring myself to think of him. He died a month ago. I found him in his bed. The others were not home. I knew where his money was. I would never have taken it while he was alive. But when I saw he was finally dead, I took it. I stole from my own brothers. And I used it to buy my ticket." He began to cry, and he came to a halt on the sidewalk. "I have to go back to the church and confess," he said. "God will punish me otherwise!"

But Aniela grabbed him by the elbow and propelled him along in their original direction, toward home, quickly. She had forgotten how Martyn could make a scene.

"Later," she said. "Think about it for a moment. Was it really such a sin to steal from them, after everything?"

"That is not for you to decide!"

"Weren't they cruel to you all along? Did they ever start treating you better after we left?"

"No. I was their servant. They made me do everything, and they paid me nothing. They treated me like a dog. Worse. They didn't beat the dog."

"So this is their punishment. Maybe it's God working through you, teaching them a lesson."

"You don't think it was wrong to steal from them?"

Aniela spat on the ground at the thought of those animals. Spitting was unladylike, but she had long since ceased to care about that. At least now she knew why Martyn seemed so guilt-ridden. It was just like him to feel this way despite the monstrous treatment he'd received. He had rope for a spine.

"You can confess this afternoon," she said. "All they would have done with the money was drink it. You know that. And they would have denied you your fair share. You know that too. Maybe you put this money to the best possible use. Think of it that way. At least in your hands it is doing some good. You're here now. You can make a new start. I'm telling you, Martyn, this country is very good to men. Learn English. Make friends. Get a job. You will get ahead."

"Really? Are the stories about America true? Is there really gold in the streets?"

"That's just an expression," she explained. For the first time, she felt like a worldly woman of the city, explaining things to a hopelessly ignorant Polish peasant. Dear God, was this how simple she had seemed when she first arrived? "There never was gold lying in the street like they say. What it means is that it's possible for a man to work hard and make something of himself, even if he comes from nothing. You can make money and save it."

"So?"

"*Tak?*"

"The police do not take it?"

"No. They are mostly honest."

"You don't have to pay it all to the landlord?"

"I own the house we live in," Aniela said calmly.

Martyn stopped again, shocked. He stared at her.

"You are wealthy?"

"No. Of course not. You see my clothes, my hands."

"Then how?"

"Jan bought it before he died. Now I own it."

"But…you are a woman!"

"Even so. Now it's mine." She wiggled her eyebrows at him in the way that used to make him laugh when he was small. "Women in America can vote, too."

Martyn shook his head.

"What a country," he said.

Yes, it was a lot to think about in such a short time. Aniela understood his confusion. Where they came from, no one owned the land they lived on or the house they lived in. It had all belonged to the noble families who dominated their world. Even if you lived in a pigsty, you could never really call it your own. And certainly not if you were a woman.

The next morning, Aniela arose before dawn to get ready for the day. She was surprised and pleased to see that Martyn was already awake. He was sitting at the kitchen table, waiting for her. She made him a cup of coffee and gave him a slice of buttered bread. He ate it gratefully. Then, after bidding goodbye to the children with the usual warnings, admonitions, and auguries of disaster should they fail to heed her words, he walked with her all the way downtown, bundled up against the cold of a late spring in Buffalo.

"You see?" She pointed to a building site, where dozens of men labored, carrying lumber and bricks. A new building was going up. It was going to be tall. "Those men are all earning good money using nothing more than their muscles. Go find the foreman and ask if you can work. If he's Polish, he'll let you. And he probably is."

"What if he isn't?"

"If he's Irish or German, forget it. They only hire their own. They will make you fight. Try another place. There are Polish shops everywhere. If there is a Polish name on the front, just go in and speak politely to them. They'll understand you. I have to go in now. I'll see you at home tonight. You'll have good luck, I'm sure."

But when Aniela came home that evening, Martyn was sitting at the table in the kitchen in the same position, as if he'd never left. Johnny was climbing on his shoulders, and Agnieszka was sitting on his lap, but he hardly seemed aware of them.

"How did it go?" she asked.

Martyn shook his head. "No luck," he said.

"None? How many places did you try?"

"I lost count."

"Did you really speak to them, or were you too shy?"

Martyn blushed. "I tried," he said. "It's not easy. I've never been to such a big city before."

"You've been to Poznań."

"Buffalo is not like Poznań."

"It's all right, Martyn," Aniela said, for she knew that his head would still be spinning for weeks after such a big journey. "No one expects miracles on your first day. It's enough that you went out and looked. I'm going to start making dinner."

"I don't want dinner," he said. "If I don't work, I shouldn't eat."

"Don't be ridiculous," said Aniela, although she remembered that phrase perfectly well from her childhood, and in fact repeated it often to herself in her head. "You can't live without eating."

"Are you really our uncle?" asked Agnieszka.

"Yes, I am your Uncle Martyn," he said. "You children speak nice Polish."

"They need to learn English," said Aniela. "Too many people around here don't learn. It's so hard. It makes no sense. There's a different rule for every time you open your mouth. I haven't said one thing right since I got here."

She regretted her words immediately, for Martyn's face became stretched with panic.

"I will never learn, then," he said. "Not if you've been here so long and can't even speak it yet."

"I didn't mean it the way it sounded. Don't get discouraged. They say that if you learn a new word every day, in no time you will understand everything." Aniela felt a new weight on her shoulders. Was Martyn going to be like a third child? She didn't have the energy to prop him up when it took so much just to keep herself going. She needed him to be able to move under his own steam, as they said here in America. As if people were trains that only needed coal.

The next day was much the same, and the day after that, and the day after that. Martyn left the house early in the morning and stayed away all day. He came home late, looking more and more discouraged. She began to wonder whether he was even trying. That Sunday at church, she learned from the other women that he'd been seen going into several Polish businesses in Black Rock, but instead of speaking directly to the owners, he merely lurked around the door for several minutes, his hat in his hands. When asked what he wanted, instead of being straightforward about it, he blurted an apology and fled.

Aniela sighed. If Martyn had ever had any manliness about him at all, it had long been beaten out of him. She would have to help him.

That Saturday afternoon, she led him into the grocery shop that was owned by Georg Stefanek, the man who had planned on going into business with Jan. Martyn hung behind her, tongue-tied. She told Georg that Martyn was a good worker and was eager to please. He was shy around people he didn't know, but he would be good at bringing out stock and finding things that were needed in a hurry. Georg looked doubtful, but Aniela did not back down. She tried very hard not to imagine that half of this shop should have been Jan's, and she tried not to think about how different life would be today if he had not died. Instead she stared Georg directly in the eye and willed him to say yes; and he did.

"You start on Monday," Aniela told Martyn on the way home. "But you really must learn to speak up for yourself."

"Thank you, Anielka, thank you!" Martyn walked straighter, and his gait was lighter, as if he had balloons tied to his shoulders. "I will make you proud. And I will pay you rent."

So Martyn worked for Georg through that spring and into the summer, and Georg said he was a good worker and gave him a raise. Aniela refused to accept rent from Martyn, but she let him help pay for groceries. He slept on the floor in the parlor, refusing her offer of the children's room for himself. He would not put anybody out, he said; he didn't want to be a bother. He had no friends and no vices, and therefore he had nothing to spend his money on. Aniela was impressed when, that June, he showed her the cash he had accumulated: nearly fifty dollars.

"What will you do with it?" she asked.

"Go into business," he said.

"What business?"

"It's a secret."

"What kind of business is a secret?"

"Well, I will tell you. But you must keep it quiet. It's a motion picture house."

"A...motion picture house?"

"Surely you've been to see a motion picture."

"Never."

"But you know they are popular."

"For people with extra money to spend."

"They cost only a dime."

"Yes, and ten dimes make a dollar. How are you going to make a business from this?"

"I have partners," Martyn said.

"So? Who are they?"

"Some friends. Businessmen."

"Do I know them?"

"No. They...go to a different church."

"What are their names?"

"I can't tell you. We have agreed to keep it quiet until we open."

Aniela became suspicious.

"You would think that if you were to open a business that needed lots of people to come, you would want to tell the whole world about it. How much money have you given them?"

Martyn became sullen and hangdog. "Never you mind," he said.

But Aniela would not give up. She kept after him until finally he admitted it: not only had he given these so-called businessmen his entire life's savings, all fifty dollars of it, but he had borrowed money from Jadwiga and Catharina as well. All told, he was giving them nearly two hundred dollars.

Aniela thought she would faint.

"Two hundred dollars!" she said. "A fortune! How could you be so foolish?"

"You are the one who is always telling me America favors bold men," said Martyn. "You have to be smart and courageous to be a success. You have to take a risk. Motion picture houses are the most popular thing now. Everyone goes to see them. It's a good idea. We are to open in a month."

"But these men whose names you won't even tell me," said Aniela. "What about them? Are they trustworthy?"

"What about me? Am I not trustworthy?" cried Martyn. "Why do you insist on treating me like a child?"

"All I want is to make sure no one is taking advantage of you!" Aniela told him. "There are bad characters here. They are always looking for a way to trick the immigrant. Are these men even Polish? Do you even understand what they are saying to you?"

But Martyn refused to answer any more questions. All he would say was that she should wait a month, and then she would see how wrong she was about him.

Aniela resolved to leave him alone for now. But she harangued her sisters, who admitted they had each given Martyn seventy-five dollars to pursue his goal. No, they did not know any more than she did about these partners of his. But he had been so excited, and they so badly wanted him to succeed in America, that they couldn't bear to turn him down.

Aniela could not be angry at them. She couldn't even name the reason she felt such dread. Maybe it was the amount of money involved. Maybe it was the secrecy that Martyn insisted upon. Whatever the cause, she waited each day for some kind of news from him, and each day he said nothing. As the one-month mark grew closer, when one would have expected Martyn to become more excited, instead he grew more and more gray in the face, and his lips pressed together ever more tightly. He would not eat. He grew snappish with the children. The one-month mark came and went, and there was no mention of any motion picture house. Martyn refused to answer any questions. He came home three nights in a row reeking of alcohol.

Aniela could not bear the suspense any more. She resolved that she would speak to him about it the next chance she got, and she would not let up until he admitted what was happening. Whatever it was, it needed to be exposed to the light of day, for she could tell it was consuming him.

But she never got that chance. Early on a Sunday morning in June, before anyone was awake, there came a knocking at the door. Aniela had hoped to sleep an extra hour this morning, but it was not to be. There on her doorstep stood a policeman. Speaking in Polish, his hat in his hands, he told her that her brother's body had been found floating downriver from the Falls. He had thrown himself into the mighty Niagara that night as horrified passersby watched. They had identified him from documents in his pocket. Aniela nodded as he spoke, half hoping that he was talking to someone else. Yet the feeling of shock and disbelief was more familiar to her now.

"Did he leave a note, by any chance?" asked the policeman. "Something to explain why he might have done such a thing?"

"He never learned to write," said Aniela.

"Do you know why he might have done it?"

Aniela sagged against the door frame for a moment. Then she straightened her spine.

"Because he was a failure," she said. "He lost money in a business."

The policeman nodded. It was a story he seemed to have heard many times before. He asked Aniela if she would be willing to come to the morgue and identify his body, just to be sure it was him. Of course that was the last thing on earth she wanted to do. But it had to be done. She told the policeman she would be there in an hour. Then she went into her bedroom and began to put on her Sunday best. Before she left, she looked at herself in the cheap mirror over the dresser Jan had bought her, and she saw that her cheeks were as dry as a desert. She had already given all her tears for her husband. She had no more left for a man who could not make it work here in this new world of opportunity, even if he was her baby brother.

12. BLACK ROCK (APRIL 1925)

Two more years went by. Everything got faster and more expensive. The children grew taller. There was a new president. Little else changed.

Aniela returned to the house after another day of housecleaning that had seemed to stretch from the beginning of time to the end of it. She'd taken the streetcar home. Her feet were raw slabs of meat, and the thought of walking two miles just to save a couple of nickels was agonizing. She could not stave off the guilt she felt over this expenditure, but there were also those days when she felt as if she could not take another step. This was one of them.

Earlier in the day she had caught sight of her reflection in a shop window, and she saw that she'd already begun to adopt the side-to-side waddle she remembered in the old women of the village. Once, perhaps, she and the other children had made fun of those old women. Now she understood why they walked like that: because their feet hurt after a lifetime spent taking care of other people.

Agnieszka and little Johnny were waiting for her when she arrived home. Agnieszka looked as if she had been crying. As usual, Johnny's nose ran freely, and his hair was wild. Aniela caught a glimpse of him like a wild animal as he poked his head up from behind the divan, their sole remaining piece of furniture. She had sold the rest to help keep the wolf from the door. At least she did not have to pay anyone to look after the children. Agnieszka was nine now, more than old enough to look after her little brother. When Aniela was that age, she had been in charge of all the chickens.

"Ma! Ma! Ma!" said Johnny. He ran in circles around her, until she put out one arm to stop him. He had so much energy it made her dizzy.

"You were gone a long time," said Agnieszka. "Johnny wouldn't listen to anything I said."

"You want the spoon on your bottom?" Aniela said to Johnny.

"No, Ma."

"Listen to your sister next time."

"Yes, Ma."

"Stop running around like that. Let me alone for a moment."

The children retreated from Aniela. They knew better than to bother her when she was this grumpy.

She added a handful of coal to the dimming pile in the stove. Coal was expensive, and it smelled terrible. But here in Buffalo you could not just go out and gather wood to burn. You could not just go out and gather *anything*. The earth offered no abundance here. You had to buy everything, and everyone charged as much as they could get away with. If they could find a way to charge you for sleep, they would soon be doing that, too. Only death promised a reprieve from the endless round of gouging that was the fate of the poor.

That was why Martyn had thrown himself into the river, she thought for the thousandth time. And for the thousand-and-first time, she promised herself that she would not think of him again.

She took some food from the icebox and warmed it in a pan. It was only kluski with cabbage, but it would fill the children's bellies enough for them to sleep. She set out two bowls for them and told them to sit down.

"Ma," said Agnieszka.

"What is it?"

"I don't like to stay inside all the time with Johnny."

"You have to watch your brother," said Aniela.

"I know, but can't we go outside? I can watch him out there just fine."

"No. You go to school and you come home. Those are the rules."

"But there are other children outside."

"We want to play," said Johnny. He rammed his spoon in his mouth and stared up at his mother as he chewed. She ran her hand over his head.

"You can play inside. The street is a dangerous place," Aniela said. "There are motorcars. There are bad men. There are wild horses running along. Gangs of wild Irishmen. Italians, with their long, sharp knives. Anything could happen to you." She almost said, *You could be kidnapped by the Prussians*, but she stopped herself in time. Fear of those people had been so deeply ingrained in her that even seventeen years after leaving the village, she still worried about them. Her Old World fears were misplaced here in America. She knew that. But she could not shed them. She had come here so that her children could grow up without that kind of fear. So why was it so hard for her to put it down? It was as if it had crept into her bones and refused to leave.

"Nothing bad ever happens to the other children," Agnieszka said.

Aniela shook her head, for she knew this was not true. There was polio, measles, diphtheria, yellow fever. There were speeding motorcars, going faster than nature had ever intended men to move. There was death everywhere.

"It's not safe," she said. "Be grateful you have a roof over your head and a bed to sleep in."

"Johnny cries all the time. He's a baby. I want to be with other girls."

"How many times do I have to tell you this?" said Aniela. "We have no one to protect us. We are all alone in the world now. So we have to be more careful than everyone else. That's just the way it is. There is no use complaining about it. It's not going to change. Get ready for bed now. No more arguing."

"Did my father die in the war?" asked Johnny.

He died right where you are sitting, Aniela wanted to say.

"Your father was a very brave and good man, and we must always keep his memory alive," said Aniela.

Her children—her two American children. They spoke Polish well enough, having learned it at her knee. They also spoke Polish with their aunts, their cousins, and the children at school. Practically everyone they knew was Polish.

But they spoke English, too, and they spoke it like natives. It amazed her to hear them ripping along as if they didn't even have to think about the words. Aniela still felt that she had to plan every English sentence five minutes in advance, practicing on the streetcar so she could say something intelligible when she arrived at her destination.

She was grateful Agnieszka and Johnny would never struggle the way she did. She was grateful they would never know what it was like to haul water from the frozen well to a house filled with men, women, children, and animals all jumbled together in a great reeking mess. Nor would they ever know the fear of a Prussian teacher, wild-eyed, spittle flecked around the corners of his mouth, belt whistling through the air on its way to destroy their hands because once again they had forgotten the proper way to pronounce the name of the Kaiser. The same Kaiser who only wanted them dead anyway, because they had committed the unforgivable sin of being born Polish. The name that to speak it brought devilish bile into the mouth and made you want to spit until your mouth was dry: *Wilhelm*.

"Ma."

"What?"

"Are we lucky or unlucky?" Agnieszka asked.

"We are both," said Aniela. "And we must pray all the time and ask God to watch out for us and keep us safe."

Because life is constantly in danger and everything good is always hanging by a thread, while the bad things in the world circle around the house endlessly, like a troop of wolves.

That morning, before she had left for work, Aniela started a new batch of sourdough.

She began by removing some of the starter from the big earthenware jar, which she had come to think of as the mother of loaves, so much bread having come from it since their arrival in this country. It was the same jar they had brought from Poland, the same one her mother had carried with her on board the ship, feeding it so that it would feed them in return.

When Zofia died, Aniela had taken over this little job. There was nothing particularly interesting about it; it was just one more chore. But something about it comforted her. The jar itself had survived this long without breaking because she had treated it like a baby. She knew that even if the sourdough died, she could start a new batch. But it would not be the same sourdough. This was still the same batch that had made the crossing with them. Some little part of it was Polish; some little piece of what was good about their homes had been carried here with the same care with which ancient people must have cupped the first spark in their hands and fed it to keep it alive, knowing that they had crossed the threshold from darkness into light, knowing that a moment's carelessness could send them back again.

She had added the starter to flour and water and mixed it well in a bowl. Then she'd let the bowl sit near the stove all day, covered with a damp rag. By some magical means that no one had ever properly explained to her, the rest of the dough took on the properties of the starter, until it too had become sour. She did not really believe it was magic, but it might as well have been. Perhaps the old women of her village had believed it was magic. A belief in magic had determined nearly everything people did, in the old days. There were spells and incantations for everything, most of them having to do with warding off evil and protecting the family from bad spirits. But you did not let the priest hear you uttering such things, because it meant you denied the power of Christ to protect you.

How did Jesus Christ and sourdough get into her head at the same time? She ought to be ashamed of herself. *Concentrate*, she thought.

Aniela replaced what she took from the earthenware pot by adding water and flour and stirring it a few times. By the same magic, the mother would grow back. You had to feed her, but she could go a long time without food. Other than that, she took care of herself.

Much like a real mother, she thought. Everything always whittling her away piece by piece, and yet somehow there was always something left.

Then she put the jar back in its spot on the tiny back porch. It didn't matter if the starter got cold. She would just get slower, the same way a person did on a cold morning. Even if she froze, no harm would befall her. She would simply wake up once warmed again. *Show me a person who can come back to life after being frozen*, Aniela thought. It was a miracle.

She put the children to bed, and then she slept. She no longer noticed how cold and lonely her bed was. She was too tired.

Aniela slept for a handful of hours. She awoke at three the next morning and stoked the fire back to life. While the coal began to heat the stove to baking strength, she added more flour to the new batch of sourdough. She kneaded the dough until it was springy in her hands. She separated it into half a dozen loaves and three dozen rolls. There was quite a lot of it. She worked quietly, so as not to awake the children, or she would have to stop what she was doing and take care of them, and then nothing would get done.

By the time Agnieszka and Johnny were stirring, the baking was finished. She had already put in several hours of work. The sun was just coming up. She gave them each a fresh roll for breakfast and allowed them a little butter. Johnny whined for jam. Agnieszka told him sharply that there wasn't any. He didn't ask a second time.

Aniela washed her face in a bowl of water that she had warmed on the stove. It was Saturday, so she had only to work a half day. Another doctor, another wealthy house in Buffalo. She recited the usual litany of warnings and threats to the children and locked them in the house. She did not look back at Johnny's wailing face pressed to the window. She, the poor Polish help-woman, would spend the morning doing the chores and taking care of another woman's children while her own sat alone in the house. In her arms was the basket containing the bread and rolls, still warm from the oven.

At least today was payday. When she was done working at dinnertime, she was handed her weekly earnings in an envelope. Inside was a worn ten-dollar bill.

"Missus," she muttered to the lady of the house. "I make bread. You want?" She could make herself understood when she had to. She held out the basket of rolls and bread. The lady lifted the cloth that covered them and smelled.

She bought six of the rolls and a loaf for fifty cents. Aniela tried to hide her delight. It would not be seemly. But this success filled her with a new burst of energy. Fifty cents was a lot of money, equal to a whole day's wages for a woman. She had already covered her costs. And she could still sell the rest to her regular customers in the neighborhood.

Profit. That was what this was. Would it anger Our Lord? Was it wrong to make too much money? Did she have any right to expect this?

Never mind. She had children to feed. Surely the Lord could not be angry with her for that.

At one o'clock, she trudged home to save carfare. By the time she returned, it was nearly two. She fed the children. Her back and knees and feet seemed especially upset with her today. She wanted badly to sit for a moment, but she was afraid that if she did, she might not get up again. She felt as if she could sleep for three days. She felt as if she was not thirty-three, but ninety-three.

Catherina and Jadwiga arrived at two-thirty, as they had promised.

"Are you ready?" they asked.

"Ready," said Aniela, starting from her half slumber at the kitchen table.

They walked down Delaware Avenue together, Aniela still carrying the basket of bread. Normally the other two would be chattering like magpies, while Aniela listened and rolled her eyes at their silliness. But today they were silent and united in their shared sense of purpose. There were big things afoot.

They stopped outside a storefront.

"This is the place?" Aniela asked. She peered in the window.

"This is it."

"And how do we know the owner?"

"He is the cousin of the man who owns the butcher shop. Kaczynski."

"He has a good reputation?"

"He doesn't have a bad reputation."

He will try to cheat us because we are women, Aniela thought. *So we will have to show him what is what.* She steeled herself for the coming negotiations.

At that moment, Kaczynski himself opened the door. He was a slight, slender man with a bewildered air, and a mustache that appeared too large for his face. Aniela had the ridiculous thought that perhaps he had borrowed this mustache for the day from a bigger man, and didn't know how to wear it. *I really need more sleep,* she thought. She reminded herself to think before she spoke, lest her tiredness make her sound like an idiot.

The man ushered the three sisters inside. Jadwiga and Catherina huddled by the door, nervous. Aniela was too tired to be nervous. She walked around, looking at the place. She also smelled it. Her keen nose told her many things that her eyes would not. It was musty and mildewed, but it had not been used to house animals in the past. That was good, at least. It had been empty for a month or so, maybe. There was no rot. It did not smell of despair or death or chaos. It was a good, clean place. He would be anxious to have it occupied as soon as possible.

"You are maybe here on behalf of your husband, *pani*?" said the man to Aniela. His Polish was not quite like hers, but she could tell he was from a small village somewhere, maybe not so different from hers.

She ignored this question.

"How much are you asking for this place?" she asked.

"Fifty dollars a month."

Aniela snorted.

"Dog's blood," she said. "Do you think I just got off the boat yesterday?"

The man appeared shocked at her bad language. "It's clean. Well looked after. A good location for a business."

"If it's so good, then why is it empty?"

"It used to be a cheese shop. The owner ran into personal difficulties. It's only been empty a couple of weeks. What business will you conduct here?"

"A bakery," said Aniela.

"A bakery, so?" The man appeared dubious. "What kind of a bakery?"

She held out the basket. "Try a roll," she said.

The man took a roll but did not bite it. He merely looked at it, as if it was a curiosity.

"People will be expecting to see food being sold here," he said. "That will work to your advantage. Forty-five dollars. "

"Maybe you think because I am a woman you can cheat me. Do you not have a mother? Sisters? A wife? Would you try to cheat them this way?"

The man's eyes had begun to roll in his head. He was like a panicked horse. Aniela did not let him see her satisfaction. Men were really no different than horses after all. If you stood up to them and made them believe you were stronger than they were, they backed down.

"I am a businessman," he blustered. "Not a charity."

"Thirty dollars a month," said Aniela.

The man opened his mouth to object further.

"We can pay you right now for the first month. Thirty dollars, in your hand. That's a lot of money. You can go home with it and show your wife. Think of how pleased she will be."

"But who will sign the lease?" the man asked. "You are women. I cannot do business with women."

"Why not? We are citizens. We can vote. We can sign documents. So we won't shake your hand. But our word is as good as any man's."

The man wrung his hat in his hands as though it was a wet cloth.

"One month only at this rate," he said finally. "Next month, if your business succeeds, we will renegotiate."

"Six months at this rate," said Aniela, "unless you want to see us fail because you are already bleeding us dry before we have opened the doors."

"You really should have brought a man with you," said Kaczynski. "I cannot do business like this. You are being utterly unreasonable."

"Try the roll," suggested Jadwiga.

The man bit into the roll that he had held onto throughout these negotiations. Aniela had expected him to like it, but she hadn't expected what happened next. He paused in his chewing to stare out into space, as though seeing people who were no longer there. Then a single tear rolled out of the corner of his left eye and down his cheek.

"My grandmother used to make bread like this," he said.

The sisters looked at each other and tried not to smile.

Five minutes later, they had signed the lease on the long wooden counter. They put it in Aniela's name, because she was the only one without a husband. If either of the other two had signed, their husbands could legally take the building from them, and there would be nothing they could do about it. They did not think either of them would do that; Catharina and Jadwiga had married decent men. But why take the chance? They were still men, after all, and Aniela had learned the same lesson enough times: if you got a man alone, you could bring out his inner goodness easily enough. But once men banded together, they were capable of acts of immense stupidity and meanness and outright cruelty. This was why Poland had had such troubles: because men were in charge.

Once Kaczynski had handed them the key and left, the sisters looked at each other. Then they looked around at the place.

"Well," said Aniela. "You know what we have to do next."

The other two nodded. They did not speak. There was no need. They had been working together all their lives, and they functioned like a piece of machinery.

They got out the buckets and mops they found in the back room, and they rolled up their sleeves.

13. KENMORE (SEPTEMBER 2015)

Approximately three million non-Jewish Polish civilians were murdered by German military forces between 1939 and 1945. Another three million Polish Jews died during that time. In total, about 20% of the population of Poland died during World War II. If this were to happen in modern America, it would be equal to the deaths of more than seventy million people.

—from Whitey Lubek's unpublished thesis

On the last night, Iggy stood at the host station, in the same position he had always assumed there: one of constant readiness. He leaned five degrees forward, bouncing on the balls of his feet, prepared to do whatever was needed: to take a coat, to shake a hand, to grab a stack of menus and say, *Right this way to your table, please.*

It didn't matter that there was no one else in the restaurant. It was dinner hour; he was hosting; therefore, he was ready. His hands remained clasped in front of his crotch, like a goalie expecting a penalty kick. When he'd started hosting, at the age of nineteen, his grandmother had always insisted on precisely this posture. She had said: "No one trusts a man whose hands they can't see." He didn't know if perhaps she worried people might think he was holding a pistol or a hidden ace of clubs, but you did not argue with Babcia. So he always kept his hands in plain sight. A smile was always plastered across his face, regardless of his mood, omnipresent but not so false as to seem greasy. People did not want to know about your personal emotions when they were eating in your restaurant. They did not want to hear your troubles. They wanted to relax, to forget their own troubles long enough to enjoy a decent meal, to be treated as special before they returned to their own lives where they were maybe not so special. You did not burden guests with your problems — even when that problem was so big it was all you could think about.

This was the fate of restaurateurs everywhere, he believed: to put their own needs last, in favor of their work. It didn't matter what was happening in the world outside. People needed to know they could depend on you to help them forget it all and enjoy a good meal. There could be volcanoes spewing lava, or UFOs strafing the streets with laser beams, but everything would be okay as long as they were still able to get the handmade pierogies they had come to know and love. In many ways, a good restaurant represented the apex of human civilization.

So, for that matter, did a good pierogi. Brownie used to make them with potato and Roquefort cheese and crumbled sausage inside. She would douse them in sour cream and sprinkle them with chives and bacon. Jesus. The world could be coming to an end and you wouldn't even notice if you had a plate full of those pierogies in front of you. Civilization could not be said to have truly ended until there were no restaurants left.

He wondered how the restaurateurs of Poland must have behaved on that first day in September, back in 1939, a long time ago now but not so long that it was erased from anyone's memory; the Poles of Buffalo had a very long memory indeed. He liked to think that if he had been there on the day Germany invaded, he would have stayed at his post as long as possible, prepared to welcome people into the place for dinner even as Stukas roared overhead, as Panzers raced across the fields, as the flamethrowers laid waste to entire villages and the fleeing families were mowed down by machinegunners. He would have continued to wait at the host station for as long as he could stand, even if no one came in, even if no one knew he was there. Maybe the people fleeing would see him there, after all, and it would help give them the strength to survive—a reason to feel that as long as Iggy Podbielski's restaurant was open, some small sliver of hope remained.

And when the gray-clad Wehrmacht horde finally appeared at his door, what then? Would he welcome them with the same equanimity, being the consummate host that he was? No. If he did, it would only be to serve them poisoned food, the filth. It would be his last act. He would not be like some, the collaborators who did not care whom they served, as long as they made money. He would fight, too, in his own way. The only way that a restaurant owner could.

But he had not been there, and his father had not been there, and neither had his grandparents. They had missed all that because Aniela had gotten on a boat in 1908 so that they could be born here instead of there. So that they could be born at all. They had missed the whole murderous shit show. It was as if she'd seen the whole thing coming. As if she'd known, despite the fact that things had been very bad for a very long time, that they were only going to get worse.

Yet somehow, he felt that he remembered the invasion. Maybe some part of him had been there after all. Maybe the memory of the Poles of Buffalo was a little too long. Maybe it was genetic.

These thoughts exhausted and enraged and weakened him, and when they came he tried to chase them away. But lately it was getting harder and harder to do that.

Maybe he needed a vacation.

So he could lie on a beach for two weeks and do nothing? He would go insane in five minutes.

He balanced on the balls of his feet and watched the traffic go by on Delaware Avenue. No one stopped. No one came in. No one glanced at the window for the glimmer of hope that seeing a man devoted to his duty might bring them. No one even knew he was there.

Iggy had been standing there for an hour when the cars pulled up.

They were very nice cars, the sort that rich men drive when they want everyone to know how wealthy they are. Ostentatious. He had never seen these particular cars before, but he knew who would get out of them: men in suits. And he was right.

They were bankers. There was no mistaking them.

There was a thin banker, a fat banker, a woman banker, and another man who did not look like a banker but more like a blue-collar type of fellow. Watching them cross the parking lot, the fat one's belly sliding over his belt buckle and all of their eyes sliding over the building in much the same way, Iggy remembered how he had always felt in the presence of the acolytes of Mammon: not worshipful and respectful, but gross and creeped out. There was something not quite human about these people. And yet they were the ones who made the rules for how his world worked.

The fat one had a set of keys in his hand. He lifted them to the outer door, but he pulled on the handle first and seemed shocked when it opened. He turned and said something to his comrades, who raised their eyebrows and affected concern. Then he pressed his hand to the glass and looked through it. Spying Iggy, he drew back in shock.

"What on earth are you doing here?" asked the fat one as they came in.

"What do you mean, what am I doing here? I'm serving dinner," said Iggy. "Table for four?" He removed four menus from the rack and waited for their response.

The bankers looked at each other. Just the three of them were in formal banker wear, including the woman. The fourth man was in a blue denim shirt and rough pants. He wore a fedora pushed back on his head.

It was Schroder.

Iggy did not know at first what Schroder was doing here. Then he realized he had a pretty good idea. He fixed him firmly with his gaze and smiled. He would not give him the satisfaction of being flustered. He would not let him know what he knew. Not yet. Schroder looked back at him, blank. So he was the anonymous buyer.

"We're not here for dinner, Mr. Podbielski," said the fat banker. "We're here to take possession."

"I see," said Iggy. "A little early, aren't you?" He looked at his watch. "The papers said close of business today."

"Right."

"Well, we serve dinner until nine o'clock," said Iggy. "We have not closed yet."

The men looked around at the empty restaurant.

"There's no one here," the thin banker observed.

"The kitchen stays open until nine, because you never know who might come in hungry," said Iggy. He allowed just enough firmness to creep into his voice to convince them that he was serious. "We always have stayed open until nine, and we always will stay open until nine, until the day we close. Even if that day happens to be today."

The three bankers looked now at Schroder, who pushed his hat further back on his head and rubbed his scalp. Evidently they were waiting for him to make some kind of decision.

"What the hell," said Schroder. "I always did like the veal here."

"Right this way, please," Iggy said, and he headed toward the biggest table, the one in the center of the dining room. He pulled out the chair for the lady banker, who looked as if she might want to object to this special treatment in front of her male colleagues, but then sat down anyway.

When all had been seated, Iggy said, "What can I bring you from the bar?"

He took their drink orders and mixed their cocktails himself: a beer for Schroder, Manhattans for the fat banker and the thin banker, and a vodka and tonic for the lady banker. He could hear them talking in hushed tones as he mixed and poured. They quieted again as he approached.

"Have you had a chance to look at the menu?" he asked, when they had all been served their drinks. "I'm sorry to say we don't have any specials tonight, and our menu is limited. But I can recommend the veal, as Mr. Schroder mentioned. Always good. The tossed garden-fresh vegetables are served with a mixture of seasonings that my great-grandmother, Aniela, invented. It brings a little something special to the dish. We do have smoked kielbasa tonight as well, served barbecued or braised." He never said "boiled." Nobody went out to a restaurant for boiled food. He took a breath and waited for this practiced speech to sink in. "And I'll bring you a dish of Kowalski's World-Famous Pickles, which have been on the menu since we opened in 1950."

"I love pickles," said the thin banker.

"Everybody loves pickles," said Iggy. "If you don't love pickles, you haven't had these pickles. They're made the same way they would have been made in the time of your grandparents. Just salt and vinegar and garlic, a little fresh dill, a grape leaf for flavor, nice and crunchy. Best pickles you ever had."

"Bring two bowls," said Schroder.

Iggy took their orders, collected their menus, and went back to the kitchen. He set two pans to heat on the stove and got a bag of frozen vegetables from the walk-in. He took out three veal steaks and a pile of kielbasa links. He turned on the gas grill and laid the sausages out to be sliced open before grilling.

It had been a long time since he'd cooked back here. He became utterly lost in his work, forgetting what night it was and who he was cooking for. When he remembered, it came as an unpleasant shock. Then it occurred to him that he could sabotage the food quite easily. He could spit on Schroder's veal. He could rub the sausages on his private parts. But what would Aniela have said about that? She would have been beyond disgusted. You served the people you didn't like with the same courtesy as the people you did like, she would have said. She would not have used quite those words, since she and the English language had never really seen eye to eye. But her general meaning would have been quite clear: Everybody Welcome. And if everybody didn't really mean everybody, then it didn't mean anything at all.

The bankers and Schroder were talking and laughing when he came out with the tray of food. It appeared that they, too, had forgotten the nature of this occasion. He seemed to surprise them when he appeared with a tray of food. Perhaps they hadn't really thought he would do it. He relished their reactions. They had expected to walk into a cold, empty place and make it theirs. He was showing them what Angela's was really all about. This was the most important meal that had ever been served here. He set their food down in front of each of them and brought fresh drinks. He also replenished the bowls of pickles, which had magically become empty.

"Mr. Podbielski, you might as well sit down with us," said the fat banker. "No need for formality."

"No, thank you," said Iggy. "I prefer to wait at my station, in case anyone else comes in."

"Do you think anyone else will come?" asked the lady banker.

"You never know," Iggy told her.

He retreated to the host station, where he stood as if waiting for more customers to arrive. He could feel their eyes on him, and he knew they thought he was crazy, waiting to seat customers who would never arrive. But he didn't care. He would rather have dug his own eyes out with a spoon than sit at that table, with the man who thought he was getting away with stealing his wife and his restaurant, and the people who were helping him do it.

Bastards.

Nazis.

Prussians.

He checked on them once and asked if everything was to their satisfaction. Don't ask more than once, he had been taught. And don't hover. Hovering makes people nervous. When they were finished, he collected their plates and brought them back to the kitchen. Then he searched in the cooler, where he found a single coconut cream pie, Brownie's specialty, only a couple of days old. It was the last pie she'd ever baked for the place. He thought maybe it should be laminated and put into a museum. But instead he cut it into eight pieces, and put four of them on plates. Then he brought them out to the table and set them down before his last guests.

"Homemade pie. Enjoy. Coffee? Liqueur?" He poured them each a cup of strong black coffee and served them a brandy from the bar. Why not? Might as well get rid of it all. Otherwise Yogi was just going to pilfer it so she could get drunk with her tattooed friends.

So. The last guests at the best Polish restaurant in Buffalo were also the people who were going to destroy it. Maybe that was fitting. This was the way of the universe. Was it not?

In his younger days, when he had been a spiritual seeker, Iggy remembered learning this lesson and not wanting to believe it. When he was twenty or twenty-one years old, he had taken a long motorcycle trip to go visit a Zen Buddhist center, which seemed silly now but which at the time seemed like the most profound and important thing he could be doing with his life. He had met a man there who told him a story:

There was a river flowing through a rich jungle, and out of the river there emerged a beautiful goddess, heavily pregnant. She was the image of life itself: plump thighs, ripe breasts, long hair echoing the river as it streamed over her belly. The goddess lay down on the riverbank and gave birth to her child: a perfect baby, born of nature. She lifted the baby to her breast and began to nurse. Then, when it was done, she devoured the baby, ignoring its cries, ripping it apart mindlessly, like an animal. When she was finished, she went back into the river and emerged again a short time later, pregnant once more, and the cycle repeated itself.

That, the man had told Iggy, was the nature of existence. Everything that was perfect would eventually become imperfect; everything that was young would someday become old; everything that was beautiful would eventually turn ugly; everything that was good would succumb to the bad. This was the way of things, and there was nothing anyone could do about it. When you tried to interfere, when you acted without thinking, when you lost awareness of the true nature of things—that was how karma was created. Karma had to be worked off. You could feel what you were feeling, sure. You were not expected to like it. And the point was not to sit there passively while someone punched you in the nose over and over. The point was that you did not take your own suffering as an excuse to cause more suffering. The more you practiced meditation and awareness, the quicker your transition through this world of suffering would be.

Maybe that was how it went, anyway. Iggy wasn't sure. The result of all his spiritual questing as a younger man was a half-remembered mishmash of Buddhism, Hinduism, nihilism, and a dash of Catholic guilt, tossed together like one of his grandmother's bowls of mixed vegetables. None of it offered a way out. There was no delivery, no salvation, no escape. Anyone who promised you anything different was selling you a lie. There was only what was in this moment, and nothing else.

And it really made no sense in the modern context. So Poles should simply have allowed themselves to be murdered by Germans? So blacks should simply have allowed themselves to be enslaved by whites? So women should just submit to men as their masters? Was that really the lesson here?

No. He did not think so. What it all came down to was that it was important to greet everyone the same way when they came into the restaurant, to serve them the same quality of food, to do the best you could, to treat everyone kindly. To make Everyone Welcome. That was their only defense against the baby-eating goddess that was existence. That, and trying to do what was right whenever possible. This was all he knew.

As strange as it sounded, even to himself, Iggy did not believe that whatever motivated Schroder was personal. Schroder didn't even know Iggy. He simply saw what he had, and he wanted it. Perhaps if it was Schroder's fault that he was going out of business, he could bring himself to hate him. But it wasn't. It was just a thing that was happening.

And hating people was exhausting. At forty-five, Iggy had come to accept this lesson, too. He preferred not to engage in hate any longer. There was so much to be angry about, if you wanted to be angry all the time. But you didn't have to be. You could choose to spend your energy on other things. Hate and anger were traps. A wise man knew how to avoid them.

Iggy watched as his guests finished their dessert and drank their coffee. Then he brought them the plastic tray that would normally have held the bill. But instead of the check, it held the key to the front door.

He set the key before the fat banker without a word. He could not bring himself to set it before Schroder. Then he headed for the door. He did not want to take one last look around. He had been doing this in his head for the past couple of weeks. He did not want there to be any ceremony at all. He just wanted to leave.

But, as an afterthought, he turned around and took the oval portrait of his great-grandmother down from where it hung on the wall. He'd nearly forgotten it.

As another afterthought, he walked back over to the table of four, held the picture up and showed it to them.

"You know who she is, of course," he said. "This is Angela. Her name was really Aniela. But she figured Angela was easier for Americans to pronounce."

He said it to all of them, but he was looking at Schroder when he said it. He was satisfied to note that Schroder appeared to have difficulty looking at him. He regarded his plate instead.

"So, Schroder," he said. "I guess you're going to buy the place. What are you going to do with it? Tear it down? Remodel it? Put up an apartment building?"

The bankers looked at Schroder, who cleared his throat.

"Well," he said, "I think I'm gonna...I'm gonna demolish it. And then I'm gonna put up a commercial property. Shops, probably. Maybe offices."

Iggy nodded. What right did he have to protest the laws of the universe?

"Well," he said. "Enjoy."

Only then did he feel the time was right for him to walk out, trying not to feel the chill that indicated three generations of ghosts were walking out with him.

As he sat in his car, preparing to pull out of the parking lot, Silvestra pulled up in hers and got out.

He turned off his engine, but instead of getting out, he just sat and waited. He hadn't been expecting to see her here tonight. He didn't think she cared.

She got out of her car and approached his. She tapped on the glass. After a moment, he rolled down the window. He could see by her eyes that she had been crying. But he felt no urge to comfort her. She could cry all day if she wanted to.

"Yes?" he said. "What is it?"

"What do you mean, what is it? It's the last day."

So she hadn't even noticed yet that he'd actually taken his things and moved out. He decided he wasn't going to tell her. Let her realize it on her own.

"Now suddenly you care?" he said.

"Of course I care. I thought I wouldn't miss the place. But I just started thinking about it and I realized what a sad day it is."

"You're drunk," he said. "Jesus, Sil. You shouldn't be driving."

"I was upset."

"You should be upset. This is the place that gave us everything. It bought our house and fed us. It's given us everything we ever had." He thought for a moment. "This is where you and I met," he said.

"I know," said Silvestra. "I remember."

He looked at her. It was difficult, but he felt it was important that he be looking at her when he said this, so that she didn't think he was beaten by it.

"Schroder is in there," he said. "He's the anonymous buyer. Looks like he wants everything that belongs to me. My business *and* my wife."

Silvestra took a step backward, as if he had hit her in the chest.

"Yes," said Iggy. "I know all about you two."

"Iggy, what? I don't know what you're—"

"Oh, don't," said Iggy. "Please, don't try to deny it. I had you followed. I had pictures taken. Why, I don't know. I needed to prove it to myself. Even though I knew."

"Iggy," said Silvestra.

"Don't," he said. "There's really nothing to say."

"But..."

"Sil," said Iggy. "The thing is, I'm not even mad."

Silvestra stared at him. Then rage crossed her face like a thunderstorm moving across Lake Erie. She stepped back, took off one shoe, and threw it at him. Iggy raised his arm to deflect it before it could puncture an eyeball. It bounced off his elbow and fell inside the car. He reached down and grabbed it between his thumb and forefinger, then held it out the window and dropped it. He realized that he was repulsed by the idea of touching something his wife's bare feet had touched. When had he started to feel that way about her? He didn't even know.

"Why not?" she screamed. "Why aren't you mad, damn you?"

"Excuse *me*?"

"Maybe if you let yourself show something once in a while, things wouldn't be like this!"

Iggy shook his head. When he was a child, he had had a temper. He used to get into infantile rages. In grammar school he'd had plenty of fights with other boys, for reasons he didn't understand at the time. Anger had simply controlled him. He was always in a lot of trouble in those days. He'd been punished on a regular basis. Eventually he'd learned to control himself, but not because of his punishments—in spite of them. And now here she was, mad at him for not being mad.

"Silvestra, the reason I'm not mad is because it died a long time ago," he said. "I'm not even sure when. You want me to hate you? I can't hate you. I was never the perfect husband. I'm sorry we couldn't have kids. I know you wanted them. I guess for me, the restaurant was my baby. For you...I don't know. I don't even know what it was. And I'm sorry about that, because I should know." He shook his head.

She stood there looking at him, one foot higher than the other now.

"Well, what now?" said Silvestra. "Divorce?"

Iggy shrugged. The very thought exhausted him. He didn't even know how you got divorced. Went to a lawyer, he supposed. Spent money. Dear God.

"Well, it may interest you to know I already moved out," he said.

"What? When?"

"See? You didn't even notice."

"*When*?"

"Today. Go home. You'll see my stuff is gone."

"Fine," said Silvestra dully.

"Look. We'll talk about it. Don't worry. I'm going to treat you fairly. Anything I have, half is yours. I won't fight you. I won't try to hurt you."

"You mean it?"

"I told you. I'm not angry."

"Then what are you?"

Iggy sighed.

"I don't know," he said. "Nothing, I guess."

She began to cry again. Then she bent over, picked up her shoe, and limp-walked back to her car.

Iggy sighed. He got out and went to her as she sat down in the driver's seat. He took the shoe from her hand and knelt before her. She swiveled to face him and he put the shoe back on her bare foot. Then he took her keys away from her, called a cab on her cell phone, and waited until it came and picked her up.

He sat there for a while after the cab pulled away. The thing was, he really had no idea where he was going. Not at this moment—he knew he was going back to his new place to go to sleep. But in the bigger sense, he was directionless, for the first time in a very long time.

When he was younger, he had enjoyed this feeling, the feeling that anything could happen. He could have ended up a movie producer in Hollywood, or the abbot of a Zen Buddhist monastery, or a heart surgeon in Poughkeepsie. Now, he felt like a tiny boat cast adrift on an ocean, at the whim of the currents, the wind, and whatever large fish might appear to swallow him whole. He knew that no matter what happened, he was just Ignatz Podbielski, whatever that might mean.

Finally, he backed the car out of its space in the parking lot.

He was about to pull out onto Delaware Avenue when a familiar car pulled in and blinked its lights at him. He sighed. Would he never be allowed to leave this place? He put his car in Park again and got out. The other driver did, too.

It was Len. In the front seat of Len's car he could just make out another figure: Mr. Danny, so small and hunched that he could barely see over the dashboard.

"Len, what'd you bring him here for?" Iggy asked. "It's over. The place is theirs now."

"Wait, Iggy," said Len. "My dad says he has one more thing to tell you."

Whatever it was, it was clearly important. Mr. Danny was struggling to get out of the car. The two men helped him out so he wouldn't fall and break a hip. They supported him by his elbows. Mr. Danny, muttering to himself in Polish, set a course for the kitchen door and began walking that way, moving unbearably slowly.

"Is he confused?" Iggy asked Len. "Does he think it's time to go to work?"

Len shrugged. "He had all his marbles an hour ago," he said. "He was pretty insistent we come down here right now. Whatever it is, he won't rest until he's told you."

So the trio of men moved toward the kitchen, at a pace that would have bored a snail, Iggy thought; but someday he would be old, too, and so he forced himself to have patience long enough to find out what Mr. Danny had to say.

14. BLACK ROCK (AUGUST 1942)

In her darker moments, of which there were plenty, Aniela gave in to the belief that the history of the world was really just a history of war, interspersed with moments of peace. The peace happened not by design, but by chance; it was almost as if every peace was accidental. As soon as the men in charge noticed there was no fighting, they started a new conflict. It seemed they could never be satisfied unless they were killing each other somewhere. But really, it was the women and children who suffered the most. They didn't start these wars, and they didn't fight in them, but they died in them all the same. They fled their homes, wept, starved, and died, and sometimes far worse tortures than these were visited upon them.

Twenty-one years after the end of the last conflict, a conflagration so terrible that everyone said there would never be another one, war had swept through Europe once more. It had begun this time in Poland. Many American people had professed surprise at the invasion of 1939, but it came as no surprise to any Pole alive. On September 1, they invaded

Poland with their Panzers, their shock troops, and their air-planes, and they had begun systematically murdering Polish people, Jews and non-Jews alike. It did not matter who you were. They simply shot you down.

For years now, the news that trickled out of that blood-soaked country had been hard to come by, and it was always bad. But Polish people had a way of learning the truth, even when it was being suppressed, and they shared it amongst each other. Entire villages were being wiped out by German troops on a regular basis. Her own village had been taken over, half of its inhabitants murdered, and renamed Kornland. This meant nothing other than "wheat field," and it illustrated perfectly how the Germans felt about Poland: it was a rich basket of food to be plundered for their own benefit. The Polish people themselves, and their history, did not matter.

The Germans came from the west. Two weeks later, the Russians came from the east, and they began doing the same thing. Once again, Poland was as helpless as a bone fought over by rabid dogs.

At least America was in the war now. They fought the Germans in Africa and Italy, and in the Pacific they fought the Japanese, who had launched a sneak attack of their own on Pearl Harbor. The Germans had betrayed the Russians, and those two countries were at war with each other. Now, on the streets of Buffalo, young men swaggered about in uniforms, their chests practically bursting with pride and patriotism. They were everywhere. She could see two of them right now from where she stood in her shop, walking down the street arm in arm, pretending not to notice the admiring stares of the young ladies, even though attracting those stares was the sole reason for their small parade to begin with.

Aniela felt no admiration for soldiers. They reminded her of the young Prussians of her childhood. They had swaggered about with the same air of pride and superiority. At the time, she had thought they were horrible monsters—and maybe they were. Now, however, she realized they were also just young men, like these. The color of the uniform made no difference. It was the same role in a different time and place. So these boys were not occupying, but defending. Still, they did not see that they were just another stone in the road of history, that there was nothing special about this time and place, and that when they died on some muddy battlefield, their bones would be pressed into the earth by the wheels of the wagons and the hooves of horses and eventually forgotten.

There was no point to any of it. People had the choice to make life about suffering or to make it about rejoicing. So why did they so often choose suffering?

And who was really more to blame for war, the men or the women? Aniela wondered as she laid out fresh loaves on a tray for cooling, the last batch of the day. It was men who made war, but it was their women who encouraged them. She knew that German wives and mothers were praising their sons for sending home trainloads of Polish produce and livestock, for slaughtering the Polish pigs who they believed had helped humiliate them after the last Great War, the one that had been supposed to end all wars. Would men even bother to make war if it weren't for the women who waited for them to bring home their plunder?

There must be some way for them to band together and stop it, she thought. If the women of the world were to agree that they would give themselves only to those men who refused to put uniforms on, war would be ended for all time within a month.

But such a thing would never come to pass.

It was all too much for one Polish-American former laundress and housekeeper, and now business owner, to think about. When her head became this busy, she felt short of breath and needed to sit down.

There were no customers in the shop at present; she pulled a stool out from behind the sales counter and sat looking out the window at the street. There was so much wrong in the world, and so little she could do about it. All she could do was take care of her own little corner of existence.

At least no more tragedy had visited them since losing Martyn. One might even say that things were going well, for the moment, although one should always be cautious and never invite the evil eye by saying so out loud.

Agnieszka was twenty-six now, married, and had just given birth to her first child, a boy. So finally, at the age of fifty, Aniela was a grandmother. And Johnny, twenty-one years old, was in the navy. To her eternal relief, he was stationed in California. Even that seemed like a world away, and it was probably populated by wild Indians who would chop your head off, but at least it wasn't the Far East. Johnny wanted to go to the Pacific and fight. Aniela prayed that he never would. She'd already buried her husband. She could not bear to bury one of her children.

The bakery was growing. She and her sisters had been here for a long time now: seventeen years. They had become a solid part of Polonia, the Polish community in America. Everyone knew the Three Sisters Bakery by reputation. It was they who provided many Buffalo Poles with their *paczki*—the stuffed yeast cakes that were so popular on Fat Thursday every year—their cheesecakes, their poppy-seed bread, their puddings and cakes, and sometimes even their candies, when Jadwiga was moved to make them. And they were also known for the hand-lettered sign in the window on a large piece of cardboard, just above the two yellow service stars, one of which was for Johnny, and the other for Danny, the little boy she had taken in when they first opened, and who was now in the Army in Europe: EVERYONE WELCOME.

The story behind that sign was complicated. Her sisters had been opposed to it. But Aniela felt very strongly that it was the right thing to do. In Germany, the Nazis had begun their campaign of extermination by putting up signs, too. Theirs had been different. Some signs warned people when a business was owned by Jews. Other signs forbade Jews from entering businesses that were owned by Christians. That had been the first step. Maybe you could say that they were only signs, that they had nothing to do with the real problem. But that was not the way Aniela saw it. The way she saw it, signs were the first symptom of the disease. The disease had grown and grown, and now there was this new war.

So the sign in the window of the Three Sisters Bakery was her way of fighting back. If those Nazi signs had started this war, maybe hers could help end it.

She knew it was nothing, a tiny gesture. But it was all she could do.

Of all the things they made, the sisters were most noted for their sourdough recipes, because they were the only ones in Buffalo who could boast that their sourdough mother was straight from the old country. By now, every Pole in the city had heard the story of how Zofia had fed the sourdough herself in the hold of that dreadful ship that brought them across the Atlantic, and how the mixture that bubbled and grew in the back of the bakery was a direct descendant of that very batch. Everyone swore that the Three Sisters' sourdough tasted more authentic, more Polish, than any other sourdough in town. Aniela herself could not notice any difference. But of course she was never going to say that to anyone. It was the thing that set them apart, that made them special. She would be stupid to point out the obvious: sourdough was sourdough.

Besides, that sourdough had allowed her to stop working in other people's homes and start working for herself. Yes, the work was hard, and the profits were slim. She kept baker's hours, waking well before dawn. She had not planned on becoming a baker, but sometimes you followed the path that was laid out for you, not the one you wanted to cut. She still walked home sometimes, to save the carfare. But she had enough money to make the monthly payments on her house, and her children had grown up with enough food to eat. A miracle, considering there was no man in the house.

Many other women in her situation would have found another husband by now. What did she need one for? If she got unlucky, he would just be another mouth to feed, another set of clothes to wash, another set of demands to meet. And she would not be as lucky again as she had been with Jan.

As Aniela sat on her stool and looked, catching her breath and trying not to worry about the state of the world, she noticed something that bothered her.

There was a woman outside in the street. She sat on the curb, holding a baby. Another child, perhaps two years old, clung to her. She'd been sitting out there for a long time. Aniela could tell by the way she was dressed that she probably had nowhere else to go. She looked to be dreadfully poor. Everyone ignored her, and Aniela knew that as soon as a policeman came along, he was going to tell her to move. Both the children were crying as they sat in the sun. It was a hot day. They would be thirsty.

If it were anybody else, someone would have stopped to ask what was wrong, and perhaps to lend a hand. But this woman was *czarny*. A *murzynka*. Black. Like the Black Madonna, Our Lady of Czestochowa. But still a woman. Still a mother.

Aniela did not think. If she had, she might not have done it. She simply acted.

She went outside and tapped the woman on the shoulder. The woman looked up, startled, guilty, and prepared to get up and move. Aniela knew the look in her eyes: exhaustion.

"Sorry, ma'am," the black woman mumbled. "I was just settin'." She gathered herself as if to get up and move down the street.

No, no. That was not what she meant. Aniela shook her head.

"You come to shop," she said. This ridiculous English language, she thought in frustration. It was like wrestling greased pigs just to get the words out.

The woman looked at her blankly.

"Come there," she said again, pointing to the shop window. "You drink water. Rest."

She practically had to pull the black woman into the place. She simply did not want to come. Aniela knew she would not be welcome in white businesses. But that was the custom of the *Amerykanski*, not of the *Polacy*. She was not one of them, and never would be. So she would give this woman some water, and if the law didn't like it, they could tell her to leave. With the world the way it was, an act of kindness seemed like the only sane thing to do.

So she sat the woman down and gave her and the child cups of water. They drank them so fast that she gave them each another.

It was cool and dark in the shop, and though it was nearly time to close, Aniela felt no urge to hurry. There were no small children waiting for her at home anymore. Later, she would go to Agnieszka's house and look after the baby. But for now, in the heat, she would just sit.

The two of them stared at each other. The baby began to fuss; Aniela nodded at her, and the black woman undid her blouse and began to nurse.

The older child had begun to fuss, too. She wanted her mother's attention. Aniela held her arms out automatically. She had never held a black child before, but she was sure it would be no different. A child was a child. The girl looked at her mother for reassurance; then at Aniela; back and forth twice more, and finally she toddled across the floor and put her head in the strange white lady's lap, where she slept.

They sat like this for a long time, not speaking.

15. KENMORE (JUNE 1980)

It's very strange, Aniela thought, how sixty years can go by so quickly. Very strange indeed.

Youth was so fleeting, and old age so...long. It seemed that one was old for far longer than one could be a child. She had been old forever, it felt. She was a grandmother many times over, and a great-grandmother, too. Agnieszka had had three children, and Johnny two; the oldest of those children had had two or three children apiece, and now the younger ones were getting married. Generations were multiplying before her eyes. It was astonishing how quickly they ceased to be babies.

And here she was, sitting alone in the living room of her house on Lincoln Boulevard, waiting for someone to come and tell her what was happening at the cemetery. If she had been capable of kneeling, she would have been at prayer right now, there on the carpeted floor. But it had been years since she'd been able to kneel. So she fingered her rosary and prayed in her comfortable chair, asking meanwhile the forgiveness of the Lord, whose suffering had been so much greater than anything she had ever had to endure.

Well, maybe. His suffering had lasted only a few days. Hers had gone on for decades, hadn't it?

She was shocked at herself for having this thought. She would have to confess it.

Aniela was not expecting any great surprises. What happened today was going to be a fairly simple thing. For sixty years, Jan had lay alone in his cold, earthen bed, with no friends or family nearby. But Aniela had purchased two plots next to each other, in a different part of the cemetery. She was having his remains moved today to their new resting place. When she died, if that blessed day ever came, they would be together again for the first time since 1920.

She hoped he would not be disturbed by the sudden intrusion of daylight into his tomb. Perhaps whatever remained of the real Jan had long fled. Maybe there was nothing to him other than dust, and he would not even be aware of this disturbance. But she asked his forgiveness anyway, just in case.

She sat like this all morning, skipping lunch. In the early afternoon, Johnny came back. Her great-grandson Iggy, ten years old, was with him.

"It's done, Ma," said Johnny, in Polish.

"Thank God," said Aniela. "There were no problems?"

"No."

"Was there...anything left?"

"His whole skeleton was there," said Iggy, who had understood her question in Polish, but could only answer in English. "It was so cool!"

"What did he say?" Aniela asked Johnny.

Johnny shot his great-nephew a warning look.

"Nothing, Ma."

"But it looked like he was…resting peacefully?"

She did not know how to express the anxiety she had felt sometimes, late at night, years after he was gone, that he had not been dead after all, and that he had woken up from some sort of coma to find himself six feet underground. One heard stories like this from time to time, and it was always horrifying. A person would need to be disinterred for one reason or another, and they would find the body twisted into a position of agony, fingertips scraped down to the bone from trying to dig themselves out of their coffin before they finally asphyxiated. No one could imagine a worse fate. Several times she had had to restrain herself from asking to have him dug up, just so she could be sure. There was a part of her that had been relieved this thing would be done, so she could put her fears to rest once and for all.

Johnny understood what she was asking. He nodded, and crossed his arms in front of him, hands folded, to show how he had found his father. So those fears, like so many others, had been groundless.

This was the father Johnny had never known, since Jan had died months before his son was born. She wondered what it had been like for him to see him that way for the first time. The years had flown so quickly that she never even thought to ask him how he imagined his father. They had only a couple of photos, hardly enough to judge a person by.

"There was something else, Ma," said Johnny.

"What?"

He took something out of his pocket and handed it to her. She took it, feeling the weight of the object in her palm before she recognized it.

It was his wedding ring.

"It was still around his finger," said Johnny.

"I can't believe it," Aniela said. What little remained of her vision was blurred by tears. "He didn't steal it."

"Who didn't steal it?" asked Iggy. He understood enough Polish to follow along.

"The undertaker," said Aniela.

She thought back to that day, surely the worst day of her life. Snow lay on the ground. She had sat in a car with her sisters, as grand as a lady, watching them carry the coffin from the house and feeling certain that the undertaker would have helped himself to the ring because she could not pay him. But he hadn't done it. He had allowed Jan to go to his final rest with that token of the fact that he had been loved, so that he would not spend eternity wondering why his wife had abandoned him in death.

Aniela was ashamed of herself. She seemed to have no control over her feelings anymore. Tears ran so freely she felt as if she was dissolving. As if she was made of rainwater instead of flesh.

"I need to go to bed," she said. "Help me, Johnny."

Johnny took her by the arm and helped her get up. He walked with her into the back bedroom, where she lay down on the bed, clutching the ring in one hand.

A thing could seem to go on and on forever, and yet when you came to the end of it, you could look back and see the whole time as one package, and it did not seem so long any more, but really just a moment. This was how she felt now about the past sixty years, from the horrible moment that she had found Jan lying on the kitchen floor, to this, when she held his ring again. As she closed her eyes, she could feel the chill of the cemetery on that frozen day, hear the rustling of her and her sisters' skirts as they stood at the graveside, hear the distantly comforting sound of the priest's voice as he chanted in Latin. It seemed to her like it had all just happened, as if time had simply compressed, and she had stepped from that moment into this one in the blink of an eye.

How strange everything was, when you came right down to it. How strange, and how fast.

16. KENMORE (SEPTEMBER 2015)

Iggy sat in his apartment above Mr. Danny and Len's first-floor home, staring at a bucket.

It was the sort of bucket you might find by the dozen lying around any restaurant, a five-gallon bucket made of food-grade plastic. It might have held flour, or corn syrup, or maraschino cherries, or ice cream. It was an old one; judging by the stains, it had been sitting at the very back of one of the fridges for a long time. No one had even known it was there. Except for Mr. Danny, that is.

Iggy was grateful the health department had never seen it. They might have had a few things to say about it.

When Mr. Danny and Len had shown up in the parking lot, with Mr. Danny going on in Polish about something important he had to show him, Iggy had no idea what to expect. Neither had Len. Mr. Danny took them first to a rarely-used corner of the place, away in the utility area of the kitchen, where a wooden cabinet stood. Mr. Danny had pointed to the cabinet with a wavering finger; he had waited while they opened it and sorted through it, looking at him for confirmation as they held up object after object, waiting for him to indicate which one he was concerned with: Was it this mop? Was it this broom? Was it this dinged-up tin platter, once used for serving cut vegetables and dip, out of service now for a decade? Was it this forgotten, dusty plastic bag of Styrofoam plates? Was it this ladle? Was it this cardboard box of broken crockery?

Aha.

When they held up the box, Mr. Danny had become visibly excited. He began to gasp and wheeze, and he shook his finger at the box with great agitation.

"Is he angry at this box?" Iggy asked dubiously.

"No, no, not angry," said Len. "It's something else. Dad, what is this old thing?"

Mr. Danny went on in Polish at some length. He had no teeth left, and he could barely draw the breath to mumble; only his son could understand him. Len listened, and whatever he heard appeared to amaze him.

"This used to be a big jar," he said to Iggy, holding his hands out to show him the size of it.

"I see," said Iggy. "Is he upset that it's broken?"

"It's an *old* jar," Len said.

"No kidding," said Iggy. "I can see that."

"This jar came from Poland," said Len, translating.

Iggy was impressed.

"Was it his...favorite jar, or something?" he asked. "Is that why he brought us here to see it?"

Len was still listening. He asked his father to repeat something. Then he turned to Iggy with a solemn air.

"This jar," Len said, "came with your family from Poland. On the boat. In 1908. With your great-grandmother. No, wait. With your...*great-great*-grandmother."

Iggy stared at the broken crockery in amazement.

"Zofia," said Mr. Danny, as clear as a bell.

Iggy picked up a piece of the broken pottery and turned it over in his hand. Whatever it once had looked like, it had been nothing special, nothing fancy. Maybe it was the kind of functional implement people used to have in their kitchens, a hundred years ago and half a world away. But it had come from a village in Poland. And they had brought it with them.

"What was in it?" Iggy asked.

Mr. Danny turned and beckoned for them to follow. Shuffling, he led them to one of the refrigerators, one which was scarcely used and which Iggy had kept meaning to get rid of, and pointed to it. Len opened it and rummaged around on the bottom shelf until he found what Mr. Danny was on about now: a large plastic food bucket with a lid. He pulled it out and set it on the floor.

"This," Len said, and he opened the lid.

Now, in his apartment, Iggy opened the lid again. He was unsure whether he was supposed to keep it open or shut. But he needed to see it one more time.

Inside was a mass of what looked like pancake batter, with a layer of liquid on top of it. It did not look very appetizing. It certainly didn't look special.

"What the hell is this stuff?" he had asked Mr. Danny, through Len.

"It's the sourdough," Len had explained. "The mother."

"The *mother*?"

"You use this to start a new batch," said Len. "That's why they call it the mother. You can pull some out and mix it with regular dough, and it becomes sour."

"Okay, so, it's sourdough."

"You don't understand. This is the same sourdough they brought with them," Mr. Danny said through his son.

"They carried it on the wagon all the way to Germany, and on the boat, and then through Ellis Island, and on the train. I heard this story a hundred times. Everyone in Buffalo knew this story. When your great-grandmother took me in off the street and gave me a job, this was one of the first things she showed me. She told me how her mother brought it with them and fed it on the ship. How she kept it going for years after that and used it in her baking. Then she started selling the rolls and the bread she made. It was famous. There were lots of other bakers, but nobody else could say their sourdough came direct from the old country. People swore it was the best sourdough they ever had, because it tasted like a little piece of Poland." Mr. Danny paused to take a quavering breath. Then he began to speak again, and Len continued to translate:

"I used this sourdough as a starter when I took over the kitchen, after that time I got drafted. After a while, we stopped doing so much baking. But she kept it going, and so did I, all this time, because you never knew when you were going to need it again, and it should be ready to go. And because it came from home. She used to say it was the only good thing that ever came out of that village. That's why I kept coming back to the kitchen all this time. I've been feeding the sourdough."

Mr. Danny reached out and patted Iggy on the shoulder, as if he was a small boy who needed consoling.

"You need it now," he said. "Take care of it, and it will take care of you."

Iggy dropped a spoonful of sugar into the mother, as Mr. Danny had instructed him. He added a little water. Then he pushed it down with a wooden spoon, stirring it gently at the same time.

The sourdough mother blooped at him.

Iggy smiled.

Once, they had owned the best Polish restaurant in Buffalo. And this was how it had started.

So maybe it could start again.

Absent-minded, he twisted the wedding ring on his finger, and he began to daydream.

17. KENMORE (SEPTEMBER 1978)

The big excitement in the family was that Little Stosh was getting married. There had not been a wedding in the family since the late 1960s, and everyone was all atwitter.

No one was more excited than eight-year-old Iggy. Being only a small boy, he had no concept of what weddings involved. He knew that they happened, he knew that he was the product of one, and he knew that the women in his family had been talking for months about dresses. Beyond that, he had no idea what they entailed. But he was very much looking forward to finding out.

Little Stosh was the younger brother of Iggy's father, Big Stosh. His name was not actually Stosh, but he looked so much like the two previous Stoshes, Old and Big, that practically every person who saw them together commented on it. Little Stosh's real name was Robert, but it had long since been forgotten by everyone, including his own mother, Grandma Aggie. And even though Stosh was his nickname, nobody called him that, either; that would really have been too many Stoshes, even for a Polish family. Instead, everyone simply called him Little. Iggy, therefore, called him Uncle Little. It was one of those things that made perfect sense to everyone in the family, and would have been impossible to explain to anyone else.

Uncle Little had lived with his parents, Old Stosh and Grandma Aggie, right up until the last possible moment, when the end of his adolescence could not possibly be delayed another second. He was now thirty years old. Everyone had despaired of him ever getting married. The Bills would get to the Super Bowl before that happened. His two main activities were working at his job as a convenience store clerk, and lying on the living room floor to watch sports on the massive, wood-encased television that belonged to his parents.

Now, however, by some miracle, he was marrying Gina, an Italian girl. A generation earlier, this would have been scandalous. It was one thing for the tribes of Europe to share a city in North America, as they had for quite some time now; it was another altogether for them to intermingle so freely. But that was the old way of looking at things. Gina was not actually *Italian*-Italian, of course. She was American, just like them, just another ingredient in the great American melting pot.

And these were modern times. The family had accepted the new way of doing things a generation earlier, when Old Stosh's brother, Sam, had married a girl from a German family, which was pretty much the strangest thing a Polish boy could do so soon after the war. And yet that had worked out all right; their children had not turned out to be baby Nazis, nor had they suffered birth defects. So maybe marrying an Italian was not so bad. They were excellent cooks, after all, and also very good at pouring cement and putting up buildings. Besides, everybody loved Gina; she had large, dark eyes and a sweet smile, and she seemed to really love Little, which was all that counted. The general attitude of the family toward this wedding, then, was one of combined astonishment and relief. It was going to be a hell of a party.

Iggy was thrilled to have been invited to the wedding. It was the first he'd ever attended. The ceremony itself was forgettable, just another interminable Catholic Mass to be suffered through, unfortunately longer than normal. But the reception afterward promised to be an event to remember.

Naturally, it was to be held at the restaurant. This was the place Iggy had already come to associate with grandeur, import, and times a-changin'. Every significant event in his family's history was celebrated there. If anything occasioned a family dinner—a wedding, a funeral, a first Communion, a baptism, an engagement, Christmas, Easter, the first day of school, the last day of school—the restaurant was where it was held. In his eight-year-old mind, Angela's was the epicenter of his family, of the City of Buffalo, and possibly of the universe.

Iggy had been allowed to help set up for the reception. He'd lent a hand moving tables, blowing up balloons, and stringing crepe paper across the doorways and around the walls. He'd also wandered through the kitchen, watching in awe as the cooks prepared a bewildering array of dishes: gołąbki, kielbasa, a giant ham, vats of soup, loaves of sourdough bread, some sort of fishy-smelling thing that he preferred to avoid, about half a dozen whole chickens, and the largest assortment of desserts and pastries he'd ever seen.

The kitchen was Iggy's favorite place. There could not be a more satisfying location anywhere. It smelled heavenly, and it was always warm, which in the humid Buffalo summers could feel oppressive—but during the other nine months of the year was comforting.

As he entered the restaurant now with his parents, some hours after the ceremony had ended, Iggy was astonished to see how full of people the place was, and how different it looked. The crowd numbered in the hundreds. Everyone was still wearing nice clothes: broad-lapelled suits in pastel colors for the men, and long, flowery dresses for the women. Uncle Little and Aunt Gina were already seated at the head table, like royalty, surrounded by their court of groomsmen and bridesmaids. The rest of the tables were a brawling, bawling mess of families, immediate and extended, young and old, fat and thin, loud and louder. It wasn't terribly hard to distinguish the Italian side from the Polish side; the Italians were all much shorter, and what they lacked in height they made up for with arm gestures and volume of speech. They also seemed to laugh three times as much. Seating arrangements were such that the two sides of the new family would be intermingled, and the wine and liquid potatoes were already flowing, which created an atmosphere of conviviality. The noise of the conversation was so great that Iggy could barely hear his own thoughts.

Intimidated by all the strange faces, he slid out of his seat at his family's table and stood by the wall, near where the band was setting up. He watched in fascination as the drummer assembled his kit, tapping tentatively on the snare drum and the cymbals and thumping the bass a couple of times with his foot. Iggy had not realized there was going to be live music. It seemed too good to be true. To his amazement, another man produced an actual electric guitar and began to tune it up. He'd never seen an electric guitar before, though he'd heard them on the radio, like in the Queen song "We Will Rock You," which always made him want to get up and dance even when he was only hearing it in his head. The drums were coated with a kind of paint that made them sparkle magically under the lights. The drummer caught his eye and smiled at him, but Iggy, shy, drew back along the wall, and out of force of habit he slid into the kitchen, where he was enveloped by wonderful smells and arms of warm steam.

He spied his great-grandmother, wearing a lavender dress with a corsage, standing with her hands on her hips and watching as the cooks manhandled a tray of pierogies onto a serving cart. Even at the age of eighty-six, it was unusual to see her not up to her elbows in something or other. He had never seen her dressed up so nicely before. Iggy knew she'd made every one of those pierogies herself, by hand, because he'd helped her. If you looked closely, you would see his thumbprints on several of the more misshapen ones.

Every time he looked at his great-grandmother, Iggy was duly impressed by how fantastically old she was. It was amazing to him that she was even alive. Everyone in the family spoke of her with extreme reverence. They all knew the story of how she had come on a ship, how she had lost her husband, how she had raised two children on her own, how she had worked her fingers to the bone to start the family business.

But all this was very abstract to Iggy. What amazed him most about her was that she had existed in that far-off and mystical time known as the 1800s. Back then there had been no cars, no planes, no telephones, no electricity, no television, no refrigerators, no bicycles, no nothing. Everything, so he understood, was made of wood, and people got around by horses. Kids did not have to go to school. There was no nuclear waste, no smog, no street gangs like in New York City. It sounded ideal to him. He regarded Aniela as a visitor from another dimension, and he wondered what she made of this dimension, where she was trapped now. He had the general impression that nearly everything about it was lacking in her eyes.

His great-grandmother saw him and beckoned him over. He came to her side and leaned into her the way he always did. She put her hand on his shoulder. He'd always thought her hands were like a man's. They were large and very strong, and heavy on his shoulder as he stood there, but he didn't mind, and the rest of her was soft.

Babcia Aniela didn't speak. It was too loud. They watched together as the food was loaded up and prepared for serving, and then Iggy went back out to the dining room and took his seat next to his mother, conscious that he was privileged enough to have been able to peer behind the curtain. None of the other people out here had been so lucky. They thought the food simply appeared out of nowhere. It made him feel important. As the food began moving out to the tables, carried by a dozen servers, he felt his heart swell with pride over the compliments that were directed his great-grandmother's way. She had not actually done much of the cooking herself, of course; everyone knew that. But every-thing was made according to her recipes, under her super-vision, and at one point in the evening an incredible thing happened, for when someone complimented Aniela on some dish or another, she turned and pointed at him and said, in her thick Polish accent: "Iggy make dat."

Everyone raised their glasses and said, "To Iggy!"

Iggy had never known such a feeling before. It made him dizzy with happiness. The feeling stuck with him for hours, persisting as he danced with one woman after another while the rock band gamely pounded on through the night. It got to be very late, and all the adults were well into the wine and liquid potatoes. Some of them were acting quite silly indeed. He replayed the moment over and over in his mind, how they had held up their glasses and toasted him, how it had all happened just so, without prompting, heartfelt, and he sensed something inside him change a little bit. He still felt as if life was a puzzle, but something important had just clicked into place.

Eventually, he crawled off into a corner and fell asleep on top of something soft. Somehow, the next morning, he woke up in his own bed, with no awareness of how he had been transported there. The whole thing seemed like a dream, until he remembered, as he poured himself a bowl of cereal and flicked on the television to watch cartoons, that moment when Babcia Aniela had pointed at him and everyone toasted him. He relived the moment over and over in his mind as he finished his cereal.

When he was done with his breakfast, he went back to the kitchen counter and put his bowl in the sink. He took a large pot from the cupboard and filled it halfway with water. He added a heavy dash of salt and turned the flame on high. Then he got down a mixing bowl, some flour, some eggs, some salt, and a little oil. He began to make kluski. He worked from his eight-year-old memory. It was a dish he had already made several times, under the supervision of Aniela. He didn't need to look it up. The recipe was encoded in his DNA. People would sleep in late and they would be hungry when they got up. He imagined that they would be depending on him for something good to eat. When people ate good food, they were happy, and everything felt like it was going to be okay forever. He would never in a million years let them down.

AFTERWORD

Although this is a work of fiction, it's based on a true story. Some of the people in this story are more real than fictitious, Aniela most of all.

Aniela was my great-grandmother's name original Polish name, and she served as the inspiration for the main historical character in this book. Just as in the story, she was born in 1892, in a tiny village not far from Poznań. She came with her mother and sisters to America on a ship called *Kaiser Wilhelm II* in 1908, when she was sixteen years old.

Over the succeeding decades, Aniela and her family encountered great obstacles, found many successes, and, like millions of other immigrant families, did their best to achieve that mythical and all-consuming goal, the "American dream." To a large extent, they succeeded.

Aniela settled first in the heavily Polish neighborhood of Black Rock. In 1915, she married Jan, a Polish man of Ruthenian descent from Limanora, Austria (now part of Poland). Both of them changed their names to sound more

American: his to John, hers to Amelia. My grandmother, Florence, was born the next year.

Much of what life was like for my great-grandparents during those early years in America is lost. One story I've heard is that, along with some business partners, John had been planning to open what would have been Buffalo's first supermarket.

But his dreams were snuffed out in an instant by a cruel twist of fate. When Amelia was pregnant with her second child, Edmund, John died suddenly of an aneurysm. The date was December 26, 1920.

The fortunes of my family were changed irrevocably. Amelia never remarried. When Florence married my grandfather, William Kowalski, Sr., Amelia moved in with them. She devoted the rest of her very long life to taking care of her daughter's house, and to caring first for her many grandchildren, then her great-grandchildren.

I don't know what my great-grandmother must have thought of the way things turned out for her. I'm certain she was grateful for what she had, and fearful of having it all taken away. Things were still hard for her in America, but nothing like what they would have been in Poland. If she hadn't emigrated, it's entirely possible she and her family would not have survived the German and Russian invasions of 1939, during which millions of Poles were murdered.

Although she chose the name Amelia, Aniela is actually translated as Angela, and everyone who knew my great-grandmother, myself included, would say this was the perfect description of her. She was a very sweet-natured woman—an angel. Much of her life was fraught with worry and fear. Yet her general nature was so soft and tender that she left an impression on everyone she met.

My great-grandmother lived to be ninety-eight years old, so there was plenty of time for me to get to know her. She was famous among us children for her chocolate chip cookies. When I was a little older, I asked her several times what her life in Poland was like. She always claimed she didn't remember. At the time, I had no trouble believing this. She seemed so old to me that her childhood must have been nothing more than a distant memory.

But I think differently now. I suspect the true answer was that she preferred to forget. Or perhaps the only stories she had to tell were not suitable for a child's ears. Why would she want to relive all that, just to satisfy my endless curiosity? There was a lesson implicit in her refusal to discuss the past: live in the moment, and don't dwell on ancient history. You survive only by moving forward.

I began writing this book partly because I wanted to imagine what would have happened to our family if John had not died on that wintry day in 1920. I imagined we might have become a dynasty of supermarket magnates, and that instead of being a writer, I might be a Buffalo businessman. But John's death was so integral to the story of my great-grandmother's life that I ended up keeping it in. Instead, I imagined what would have happened if her home baking had been transformed, little by little, into a business.

I also wrote this book because I wanted to get to know my great-grandmother better. She passed away in 1990, eighty-two years after coming to America. I've thought about her nearly every day. (This is especially true when I'm making egg noodles or pickles in my kitchen in Nova Scotia, Canada, where I live now.) Her wedding portrait hangs in our home, in an antique oval frame. I will never know as much about her as I would prefer, but at least I can imagine.

There is one other part of this story that's true. That's the story of the ring John wore on their wedding day in 1915. He was buried with this ring on his finger in 1920. In 1980, my great-grandmother purchased adjoining plots in St. Stanislaus Cemetery, one for him and one for her. She had his remains disinterred and relocated to the new plot, in preparation for the day when they might rest side by side again. When the cemetery workers finished digging up his grave, they saw that the ring was still on the finger of his skeleton. The decision was made to remove the ring and return it to Amelia, who by then had been a widow for sixty years. She was amazed that the undertaker hadn't stolen it before burying John, because she had no money to pay him. Later, she gave the ring to my father, who presented it to me the day I married my wife in 2002. It's a plain, thick, heavy gold band. I don't wear it often, because I'm terrified of losing it. But the inscription inside is still plainly visible: *A.L. to J.C. 6-16-15.* It's my most treasured possession, and I look forward to passing it on to the next generation someday.

As the descendant of immigrants from Poland, Ireland, and Germany, I've often felt ashamed of how soft and easy my life in America and Canada has been. I have to remind myself that this is the reason they emigrated in the first place—so that their descendants would not have to suffer as much as they did. I don't think many people my age or younger have a clear idea how hard life was for our ancestors, just a couple of generations ago. All of them endured hardships that would have put us on a therapist's couch. All of them played an important role in making our society what it is today.

But I feel a little more complete now that this book is finished.

Thank you for taking this journey with me. I hope it inspires you to make your own journey of self-discovery, wherever it may lead.

William Kowalski

ACKNOWLEDGEMENTS

Thanks are due to my father, William Kowalski; my mother, Kathleen Siepel; my uncle, James Kowalski; my aunt, Mary Skorupa; and my first cousins once removed, Antoinette Miranda and Suzanne Lema, for their assistance in sharing memories, photos, and documents about my great-grandmother.

The publication of this book was made possible by the generosity of over one hundred contributors to a campaign conducted on Kickstarter.com to fund production and publication costs. Their names are listed below, in alphabetical order. The author wishes to thank them deeply for their support, without which this book would not exist in its current form.

Andra Abolins

Liz Ahl

Ethan Allen

Andrea

Kay Aram

Villi Asgeirsson

Janet Balsom

Janet Barkhouse

Clara Allmond Zurn Belli

David Beltran

Tim Benacci
Karen Berry
Keith Blyth
Julie Boam
Juergen Buerger
Lynn Craker
Dale Clark
Dawn
Marq de Villiers
Kellie Doucette
David Duncan
Theodore Enders
Nathan Eppler
Janice Fatica
Lynn Feasey
Melissa Firestone
Scott Fotheringham
Jimmy Fountain
Mary Ann Frew
Sarah Gilson
Kathleen Glasgow
Mark Gowdy-Jaehnig
Brian Greene
Jim Hansen
Helen Harwell
Cara Herbstritt
Michael Higgins
Beth Hoar
Glenna Jenkins

Jenna
Alisa Johnson
Juditha
Albert and Janina Juszczak
Karmen Kohl
Asia Miller Kowalski
Bill Kowalski
Joanne Kowalski
Lisa Kowalski
William Kowalski
Krishnan
Rebecca LaSalle
Mike Layne
Suzanne Czamara Lema
Ben E Lewis
Roxanne Lindsay
Jay Lipsitz
Keir Lowther
Peggy MacKinnon
Julie Marron
Kim McCarron
Dan McCloskey
Miranda McEvilly
Mark Stephen Meadows
Megan Megan
Raina Mermaid
Antoinette Miranda
Chris Mraz
Susanne Nedergaard

Mo Neff

Dave Nolan

Kelly Norman

Sean Norman

Bethany O'Connell

Scherri Olivella

Frances Owen

Jessica Patten

Pamela Purves

Dr. Juneau Robbins

Noah Rosenstein

Alex Ruttenberg

Patricia Ryan

Karen Schaffer

Kristin Schreel

Adam Siepel

Ginny Siepel

Kathleen E. Siepel

Kevin H. Siepel

Mary Skorupa

Philip Slayton

Alison Smith

Susan Pietras Smith

Susan

Stella Vaccaro

Amy Walsh

Bailey Walsh

Russell Wangersky

Luke Warren

Lloyd Williams

Ellen Wiseman

Michael Zinanti

Richard Zimler

I thank Artur Dobrowolski for his assistance in the translation of official documents, and for verifying details about the region of Poznań. I also thank Keir Lowther for his comments on an early draft of this book.

PUBLISHER PROFILE

Philip Dregalla is one of the publishers of this book. Born and raised in Erie, PA, Mr. Dregalla attended Cathedral Preparatory School for Boys and the University of Pittsburgh. Afterward, he embarked on a career in financial services, and later in financial software sales, before investing in real estate and his own business. Now the owner of a transportation company, he is currently a resident of Akron, OH, where he lives with his wife, Lisa. His generous contribution towards the publication of this book is greatly appreciated.